FOLLOW IN MY FOOTSTEPS

D.J. WADDISON

Copyright © 2023 Daniel J Waddison

All rights reserved.

ISBN: 9798370267796

To the person who found this book, enjoy!

DJ Waddison

D.J. WADDISON

FOLLOW IN MY FOOTSTEPS

DEDICATION

Dedicated to; my late friend Jalen who we lost too soon, Grandad Len – I wish you could see me now and all I have achieved, to my loving parents who have supported me and pushed me to always do my best, and to the friends and colleagues who have supported and encouraged me to get this finished.

I love you all.

CONTENTS

	Acknowledgments	i
1	Once a Bully	1
2	Life Goes On	17
3	Reunited, But Not United	31
4	Tensions	47
5	A Friendship Blossoming	61
6	Ruined	70
7	Maintaining The Lie	82
8	Pushing Away	96
9	Caught	109
10	Fate of a Friend	127
11	Double Whammy	138
12	Looking Up	154
13	Heads or Tails	167
14	Ryan	176
15	Jane	191
16	Condolences	199
17	Wanting The Truth	213

18	Fred and Olly	225
19	Jason	232
20	Reece	242
21	That's How it Happened	250
22	Epilogue	254

ACKNOWLEDGMENTS

Firstly, I'd like to thank my mom and my dad. I couldn't be the person who I am today without them. They've always been in my corner pushing me on and supporting me in ways which, at the time, I didn't even notice. When I've been down at my worst, they've been there. I love you both.

I'd also like to acknowledge my friends and colleagues as well who have been there and have given me the boost and support I needed whilst writing this book. They've helped me with proofreading and general support when writing it as well. Thank you for your support and your honesty.

I also want to thank my "G.MA" for always making me smile, and believing in me, no matter what.

I also need to thank my friend Blair for helping me with the cover of this book. He modelled the cover for me which was a massive help to getting the book ready.

The people mentioned have always seen the best in me, even when I've been miserable and down in the dumps, they've given me the boost to get out of that dark time. Writing a few words in a book to say thank you doesn't even cover the support that I've received.

I also want to say a big thank you to all the local businesses who have supported my book by putting out flyers and advertisements in their shop windows. The support has been incredible, so thank you.

Finally, let me thank everyone who has bought this book and is taking time out of their day to read it. Your support means a lot. Even though most of you I'll never meet, thank you from the bottom of my heart.

I hope that this book meets everyone's expectations. I've put a lot of work, time, and effort into it.

Enjoy!

1 ONCE A BULLY

This story is one of tragedy. Of love and loss. Smiles and tears. Happiness and sadness. But this story is different. For this tells the story of unlikely friends. But to really start this story, we need to go all the way back to the beginning. Back to the days of Alien Slime Eggs, questionable hairstyles, and movie renting stores for when people used to use VHS tapes. If you had not guessed it yet, this story goes all the way back to the nineteen-nineties.

The year is nineteen-ninety-five, and a thirteen-year-old Jake Lawson was celebrating his birthday. Jake had to celebrate his birthday at school though. It was not much of a celebration for him. The morning and the evening would be different, but his day would remain the same.

He rushed downstairs like an excited child at

Christmas and opened his cards and presents from his parents and family. Jake was so excited for this day. His mother packed his bag for him, gave him a kiss on his forehead and sent him on his walk to school.

Jake had to walk for about twenty-five minutes. He timed it once on his wristwatch out of curiosity. He knew exactly when to leave to get to school for the bell ringing. The less time he spent there the better. It was a nice peaceful walk through the forestry area for him. That was until a plastic bottle come from out of nowhere. The half-empty bottle of water hit him across the cheek. This knocked Jake off balance, but he was still standing strong. He brushed it off and kept on walking. He pretended not to hear the laughter coming from Reece and his 'cool' mates behind him. Jake didn't think they were very cool, but everyone else seemed to.

Jake carried on walking and another bottle hit him to the back of the head. This time, the bottle was only a quarter full, so it didn't hurt him as much. Again, standing strong, he pretended not to notice and carried on walking. At this point, Jake was feeling upset. After all, it was his birthday, and he was being bullied before the clock had even struck eight.

He walked for five minutes whilst being pelted with bottles, stones, and pretty much anything the little shits could get their hands on. Jake was timid and patient though. Plus, he was used to this. He knew a little alleyway coming up on his left he could run down and hide. There were a few alleyways which he knew where, if he held his breath, they would not find him.

So that's exactly what he did. Jake took a left and ran instantly. He could hear the pounding of footsteps of five people coming up behind him.

"He went down this way!" Reece shouted, "Weirdo likes hiding in the dark."

"Just leave it Reece, we'll be late. It ay' worth it for him." Ryan shouted.

"Oh, it definitely is. Did you know it's his birthday today? He owes us his birthday digs." That was Reece again, shouting loud enough that the whole cul-de-sac next to the alleyway could hear.

Reece was the only one who followed Jake into the alleyway. He walked around for a minute, stepping on twigs and branches. For Jake, it was the longest minute of his life. He felt like he was in that dinosaur film where they had to be super quiet to avoid alerting the feared Tyrannosaurus Rex. Except this was the Tyrannosaurus Reece.

Reece slowly walked out of the alleyway and walked off laughing boisterously with his friends. Jake waited in there for five minutes before coming out, checking left and right to see if it was clear. Then he carried on his walk to school.

The nightmare didn't end for him there though. All day, Jake was harassed by Reece and his gang of friends.

They used to roll little pieces of paper into plastic straws and fire them at his head. They took his homework off him in class, which got him detention with the teacher for not doing the work. They would push, punch, and kick him whenever they got the chance. Those things all happened in one day. His birthday. There was no difference though for Jake. This happened to him every day.

Luckily, because of the detentions he would get for his 'missing' homework, it meant that he often missed them on the walk home. This was his chance to get peace and quiet. Instead, he would spend the walk home letting out the tears that he had been holding in all day. His life was made a living hell by Reece and his mates. Luckily, he always bought an extra packet of tissues with him for the walk home so he could clean himself up in time for when he walked through the door. This was to put on a brave face so that his parents didn't suspect anything was going on. He couldn't tell them how bad it was. They would be straight up the school complaining, which would make things worse. He couldn't move schools either, as he moved from the last one for the exact same reason. Instead, Jake put up with it every day he was at school. Putting on the brave face was the hardest part for him though. He was a clumsy child, so it was easy for him to explain the cuts and bruises.

Jake kept this up for years. He could slowly feel himself getting closer to his breaking point every day. He would try to display a brave face. However, deep down, his frustration and anger continued to grow. Rooting itself deep in Jake like a tree.

Day after day, he was tormented by these bullies. Jake knew he had to be the bigger person though. After all, if he reacted, he would just sink to their level. That's what his mother used to tell him. He didn't want to be like them. Not at all.

Jake was bullied non-stop for the next few years. Every day for Jake was the same hell caused by the same people. Every minute was a nightmare for him. A nightmare that he could not seem to wake up from.

Skip forward some years, to the year nineteen-ninety-eight. Jake was sixteen now. The years had passed, but the bullying continued. The only breaks that Jake got were the school holidays.

It was his final year of school. It wasn't long until he could follow his dreams. He wanted to move into writing. He was always good in his classes and wanted to be a journalist. He was a paperboy at the time, trying to get his foot in the door. It also gave him the chance to read news articles and look at the structure.

He would spend his spare time reading newspaper articles and creating his own absurd headlines. 'Monkey lands on the moon', 'Penguin spotted in local park.' Headlines that he knew were not true but just added comical relief to writing the articles. He wanted his pieces to incorporate humour, so the readers could connect with the story they were reading. Nobody read his stories though. Just his parents.

Jake had about two weeks left of school. He was sitting his exams. He had done four of them so far and only had a handful left to go before he could say goodbye to his dreadful school years.

He was walking in one day as there was a study class on for anyone who wished to attend. Jake's walk started out as a nice, peaceful, walk. Today he wasn't expecting any trouble. After all, Reece and the other lads hadn't bothered showing up for any of the other study classes. Jake was actually able to enjoy his walk for once. He listened as the birds chirped on in the trees' which surrounded him.

About ten minutes before he was due to get to school, Jake heard a kicking sound in the distance. He tried to think of what it could be. Before he even realized, a football hit him straight across the back of the head. The ball hit him with enough force that it managed to knock his glasses off which caused them, and Jake, to fall to the floor.

Just then, he heard footsteps approaching. He knew exactly who it was. It was Reece and his mates. Nothing had changed over the course of those few years. After all, once a bully, always a bully.

Reece stood on Jake's glasses, causing them to crunch and shatter under his black size nine sneakers. Reece looked Jake in the eyes as he twisted his foot left and right on Jake's glasses. He lifted his foot to reveal the broken glasses in bits on the floor. Jake looked up in anger. He went to get up.

"YOU-" Jake didn't get a chance to get his words out. Reece pushed him straight to the floor. It was a good job really. His parents had raised him better than to swear. Jake's bag fell off his back and Reece's friend Fred picked it up. He and the other friend, Olly, emptied the contents out and turned the bag inside out.

Jake went to get up again, but Reece pushed him straight back down. He stood over Jake and knelt down. Then, he punched Jake straight to the eye, causing him a sharp pain. Jake dropped onto his back.

Reece gave a nod to the other boys with him. Ryan Green, Fred King, Olly Foster, and Jason Moore.

They all started kicking him. Jake curled up into a fetal position, making sure to protect himself as much as possible. With every kick, he felt something else crack. Thirty seconds later, they stopped. Jake opened his eyes slowly and saw a hint of light shining off a long, thin object. Jake felt weak, but beneath that, another feeling emerged. One that he had not felt before. Rage. He reached out and grabbed the object, not knowing what it was. He sprung to his feet and swung the metal bar towards Reece. Reece ducked and Jake closed his eyes, waiting for the punch that never landed. He felt something stop the bar. A thud.

Then there was silence. The sound that followed was the sound of someone, or something, dropping to the floor.

Jake opened his eyes to see Ryan lay down on the floor unconscious. Blood was pouring from a fresh wound on the left side of his forehead. Jake couldn't believe what he had done. He froze. It was now going to be fight or flight. Reece was in his way whilst the others rushed to Ryan's aid. Jake checked his watch. He had fifteen minutes before his study was due to start.

"You're not going anywhere you prick." Reece said with anger in his voice but a smugness to his face.

"I'm sorry. Please, just let me go." Jake responded, with a whimper in his voice, still holding onto the bar which was now stained with a few drops of Ryan's blood.

"You might need that." Reece pointed at the bar in Jake's hand as he rolled his sleeves up. Fight it was. Reece approached Jake, fists clenched, shoulders and arms swaying. Jake didn't think, he thrust the bar straight to Reece's chest, winding him. This gave Jake the perfect chance to throw an uppercut and put Reece on the floor with Ryan. Jake didn't do that though. Instead, he ran past Reece, letting go of the bar and sprinting all the way to school.

He walked into his study class, not saying a word. He'd left his bag there, so he had to go to the back of the class and grab a pen and a notebook to make notes. Everyone in the room stared at him. Jake didn't realise how he looked. He was covered in gravel dust, dirt, dried blood, cuts, and bruises. His shirt was ripped, as were his trousers. The teacher, Mr Shaw, looked over at Jake and couldn't get the words out of his mouth.

"I really wish that people knew to put their dogs on a lead. Some rottweilers just legged me over chasing after its Tennis ball." Jake exclaimed to the class. The class fell silent for a moment and then burst into laughter. Mr Shaw did not look impressed though, nor did he look angry. He looked concerned. You would too if a student walked into your class in the state that young Jake was in.

Study was for two and a half hours. Jake's was cut short. Three knocks on the classroom door changed everything. Mr Shaw opened the door to see two Police Officers standing outside. Mr Shaw stepped out and shut the door behind him, whispering with the officers. Jake was on alert, and people were noticing.

"I may have kicked the rottweiler as I tripped over it," Jake said, trying to make humour out of the situation. This time, nobody laughed. The gravity of the situation set in. Jake remained in his seat until the door reopened. To no surprise, Mr Shaw called for Jake to come outside with his belongings. Jake didn't have anything with him, so he just left with his head down.

He stepped outside, trembling, and looked up at the two Police Officers standing before him. Both officers were male. The one on the left had more of a grizzled look to him. Scruffy beard, a stocky build and a tattoo on his arm which was on show because of his rolled-up sleeves. When Jake looked into his eyes, he saw nothing but cold. Jake felt like he was another one of the problem young criminals that the officers had been called to deal with. The officer on the right, however, was different. He was clean-shaven, with a more sympathetic look in his eyes. He must have been new.

"Jake Lawson?" The officer on the right asked, confirming if he had the right person.

"That's me, sir, before you say anything let me explain-" Jake's sentence was cut short. It was clear to Jake, Mr Shaw, and the officers what was about to happen.

"You're under arrest for an assault on Ryan Green. You do not have to say anything, but it may harm your defence if you do not mention, when questioned, something which you may later rely on in court. Anything you do say may be given in evidence." The officer on the left said, grabbing a hold of Jake's hands and putting them behind his back in handcuffs.

Jake was beside himself with worry. 'What are my parents going to think?', 'I didn't do anything wrong', 'I was defending myself', 'Surely they'll see that, right?' These were all thoughts going through Jake's head. Every other sound was just numb to him.

The officers walked Jake to the Police car, where they sat him in the back. Once he was buckled into his seat, the officers then started driving to the local station.

Jake was put into a cell and, for the next few hours, the four walls of the cell became his best friends. The cell was a small, cold space which was only being made cooler by the breeze coming from under the door. He got to speak to his mom but couldn't tell her what was going on.

"I'm sorry mom. I shouldn't have reacted. I'd had enough." He said on the phone.

"We'll talk about it when you get home, I'll be waiting for you at the station." Jake's mom responded. She had that tone of disappointment in her voice. That was worse than her being angry. She was disappointed.

An officer took Jake out of his cell not long after and showed him to a room and directed him where to sit. She loaded up the cassette recorder and hit record. The first part was a blur.

"Jake?" The officer said, "Are you going to answer me or sit there quietly?"

"Sorry. What was the question?" Jake responded softly.

"What happened between you and Ryan? I can see you're covered in cuts and bruises, but that doesn't tell us what happened." The officer asked Jake. This was a different officer from the one who arrested him. This officer actually wanted to listen to what Jake had to say.

"I hit him." Jake replied bluntly. Not offering any other explanation.

"With this?" The officer pulled out a bag which had a metal bar inside, identical to the one Jake used earlier on to incapacitate Ryan. Except this one had more blood on it than Jake could recognise.

"I think so, yeah." Jake replied bluntly again. He didn't want to relive the moment. He just wanted to move on. He wanted to be punished for his actions, as he knew he shouldn't have hit Ryan.

"Were the boys bullying you? We can help you if they were. You're not going to be in trouble for standing up for yourself Jake." The nice officer responded, putting their hand on Jake's arm to comfort him.

Jake wanted to tell the truth. However, he knew that if he did, he would get out of the punishment which he felt he deserved for hitting Ryan.

"Nope. Their ball hit me, I lost my temper and grabbed the bar. Then I hit him." Jake told them. He wasn't lying, he was just holding back the truth.

Knowing that she wouldn't be able to get anything further out of Jake, the detective ended the interview. Jake was put back into his cell for another hour.

Eventually, Jake was released on bail with conditions not to contact any of the boys involved in the incident. That wouldn't be an issue anyway. By now, Jake hated the sight of them. His mom was waiting outside. He walked straight to the car, opened the passenger door, and got in. His mom looked at him for a moment and then hugged him.

"Did you tell them the truth?" She asked in a caring, motherly voice.

"Yeah. I did." Jake said back, wiping the tear from his eye that was beginning to form. His mother put her hand on his shoulder for a moment. A touch which comforted Jake. A mother's love.

She put the car in gear and began to drive home.

FOLLOW IN MY FOOTSTEPS

Nothing else was said on the drive home. Jake got in and went straight to his room. He stayed in there all evening and night. He came out when his parents went to work. He didn't want to speak to them, as he knew he had let them down.

Dread and worry filled Jake's head as he waited and waited for news on what would happen next. Weeks passed. Then, Jake received a notice in the post. A warning. He was going to court.

The trial took place over the course of two days, where Jake told the court what had happened and came out with the full truth. He was sentenced to three months in prison, which felt like forever.

Jake was on his best behaviour in prison. It was tough for him. He couldn't make any friends and once again found himself being bullied. He was different to all the other inmates. Some of them were in for serious crimes. Robbery, grievous bodily harm. Jake was only in for actual bodily harm after it got lowered from the more serious offence. The judge had taken pity on him though.

Jake was out in the exercise yard one day. Minding his own business as he usually did. He stood and kicked a stone around in the corner, trying to stay out of any trouble. Yet somehow, trouble still managed to find him.

A group of four young lads approached him. All of them were much bigger than him in stature. They weren't massive but they weren't small either. All of them were sporting either clean-shaven heads or buzz cuts. Jake didn't know what he had done but they didn't look happy.

"Hi guys," Jake said sheepishly, "Everything okay?"

The four lads shared looks between themselves for a moment. Then, the one who was front and centre spoke up.

"This is our spot." The lad said to Jake.

"Sorry," Jake replied, picking up the stone he had been kicking around, "I'll move."

As Jake went to walk away, one of the other lads put their hands across his chest, stopping him from taking another step. Jake gulped.

"I'm going," Jake told them, "Please, just leave me alone."

Out of nowhere, Jake was pushed to the hard concrete floor. His head went fuzzy as it hit the ground. The lads started to kick and stamp on Jake over and over again until five guards ran over and grabbed hold of all of them.

Jake had received the message loud and clear. That was their spot. He wasn't welcome there.

He was taken back to his cell. The warden came and saw him shortly after and Jake was able to explain his version of events. He was the only one with injuries after all, so it didn't take a genius to figure out that Jake was the victim of a meaningless beating.

Jake didn't fight back against them though and kept up his good behaviour. As a result, Jake was allowed out to do jobs in the prison.

FOLLOW IN MY FOOTSTEPS

He was cleaning the toilets one day when a fellow inmate approached him. He tapped Jake on the shoulder. When Jake looked up, he saw a boy standing before him. This boy was only seventeen but was built like a thirty-year-old wrestler. Jake thought he knew what was coming. It was going to be another beating for being 'different' to everyone else.

"You're not supposed to be here," The inmate said to Jake.

"Sorry, I was asked to clean but I can come back later." Jake picked up the mop and went to walk out, keeping his head down. The inmate grabbed his arm. Jake took a gulp and looked back at the inmate.

"What's your story?" The inmate asked Jake. This caught Jake by surprise. He'd seen this inmate before hanging around in the tough crowds but could not recall ever seeing him fight anyone. Fights were a regular occurrence too, so maybe this inmate was different. Or maybe Jake was to be this prisoner's initiation into a gang.

"It's a long story." Jake responded, surprised by the question he had been asked. "Why do you want to know?"

The inmate paused for a moment and looked Jake up and down. He put his hand out to Jake and prompted him to shake his hand. Stunned, Jake put the mop down and shook hands with this giant. Suddenly, the giant didn't seem so scary.

"A lot of people want to hurt you. I don't know why. Maybe it's because you're different. You don't deserve to be here. I can see it and so can they." The inmate said to Jake. "You're with me now, my names Eric."

"Thank you, my name's Jake." Jake replied, still shocked by the interaction. Eric then walked out of the toilets and off to the area he had been tasked to clean.

Jake was confused by the interaction. He didn't know whether to trust Eric or whether to keep his guard up.

One thing became apparent though. Once word got around that Jake and Eric were friends, nobody bothered to mess with Jake again. The remainder of Jake's time in prison was somewhat peaceful. He didn't enjoy it but at least he had a friend. Someone who could watch his back. Shortly after, Jake was released into the real world again. Free at last.

When he got out, he got a job working at a local paper company in the print room. He didn't tell anyone about him going to prison. He never wanted to tell anyone. It was a secret he swore would die with him. He kept himself to himself and stayed out of everyone's way. He was still quiet, but the short time in prison had changed him emotionally in ways which he just didn't know yet. At the moment though, Jake was almost where he wanted to be and was trying to get his life and career aspirations back on track. One thing he didn't lose in prison was his love for journalism, a love that he sustained when he got released back out into the real world.

2 LIFE GOES ON

Two years passed of Jake being in the print room. Eventually, he made it out of that confined space and up into the offices where he began to learn the art of journalism. Jake helped contribute to a few big stories and sometimes got to write a piece of his own. Most of his job was just conducting interviews with members of the public who had some bizarre stories, much like the ones which he used to write about in his fantasy newspapers.

Jake waited for his shot to be able to write his first big story, but nothing came up. He watched, learned, and listened to what the other writers were saying and doing. Jake did that for six months. One day, an idea came into his head. A story which he thought, if told right, could shoot him up the ranks. Jake knew what he had to do but he would have to go behind his boss' back to do it. Jake needed to go back to prison. Jake needed to see Eric again.

Jake would visit Eric on the odd occasion. He was the closest person Jake had to a 'best friend.' Eric was like the older brother that Jake always wanted, apart from the whole being in prison part. Jake didn't feel comfortable being in the prison and Eric understood that, so Eric knew Jake wouldn't be able to visit as much. Jake sat down at the table and waited for Eric to be escorted through. Eric came through the doorway, approached the table, shook Jake's hand, and sat down.

The two had a brief catch-up over a few things. Jake didn't have long to speak to Eric, so he had to get what he wanted to say out into words quickly.

"Eric, I want to write a story about you. About the reason you're in here. To show that not everyone in prison is a monster and that everyone deserves a second chance." Jake said to Eric. Eric looked back at Jake with a smile on his face. This was a smile of pride. Not just any pride. Brotherly pride.

"I'd love to do that Jake, but I can't. Some of the guys in here wouldn't appreciate it." Eric replied, putting his head down, worried that he had disappointed young Jake. "Besides, my story isn't worth telling. It's not one that I'm proud of."

Jake was gutted. This was his shot, his best chance to boost his career, and it flew straight past him. He couldn't let Eric see that though.

He didn't want to put any pressure on Eric. Plus,

beneath all the muscles, Eric was one of the nicest guys Jake had met. Jake nodded his head.

"I understand, it was worth an ask." Jake closed his notebook and put it into his rear trouser pocket. Eric looked at Jake and saw this wasn't just about himself. Jake needed this.

"Why me, can I ask?" Eric asked Jake.

Jake responded to Eric, "I don't know your story. I came into prison as a scared young boy. I didn't know what to expect and just assumed everyone would be out to get me. The day that you approached me, I was scared as shit."

Eric interrupted Jake with a chuckle, "Sorry, carry on mate." Jake smiled.

"You have shown me though that not everyone is the same. Not everybody is out to get me. You have shown me that beneath the tough exterior, there's a polite and caring person who just wants to look out for the little guys like me." Jake wasn't talking to Eric as a journalist but as a friend. Eric could see that.

Time was coming to a close for Jake, and visiting wasn't for another week. Eric needed some time to think about the story. He didn't say anything to Jake, he didn't want to disappoint him for a second time. They shared a few more jokes and short stories and then Eric was called to go back in. Eric walked back with the warden to his cell. Jake went out to the car park and waited for his taxi. He couldn't afford a car. Not yet anyway.

Jake tried and tried to get the story idea out of his

head and think of another one, but he couldn't. He had got writer's block before he had even started writing. Maybe the journalist life wasn't for him after all. He couldn't get a good story or an opportunity to tell one. Jake spent the rest of the week thinking of ideas for new stories, but nothing came to mind. Another week passed and a letter came in the post addressed to Jake. It was from Eric.

'Jake, I've had a change of heart about the story. Come visit me when you can, and I'll give you your first story. From Eric.'

It was a short note, but it confused Jake all the same. Jake hadn't told Eric that he planned on making him his first story. Eric must have figured it out himself. Either way, this could be Jake's chance. He went to the next visiting day to see Eric. Even out of prison, Eric was looking out for him.

Jake waited in the visitor's room. Eric came in and sat down with a smile on his face. Without Jake saying a word, Eric spilt his guts.

"Nineteen-ninety-six. August twenty-eighth. I was skipping school one day with a group of my friends. Thought it was the cool thing to do back then. There were about six or seven of us. Due to our mass in numbers, we could do whatever we wanted. We felt powerful. On top of the world. We all went to the same school, so we all ditched it on the same day. This day was going to be different though. We'd always talked about making money. Quick money to spend on cigarettes and booze. There was an off licence near to the park we used to hang around in. We didn't really have a plan. Balaclava up and use our mass in numbers to strike enough fear into the shopkeeper that he would hand over his cash out the till.

We ran in, trying our best to be bold and intimidating. Two of the lads instantly went around the counter and pulled out knives. The shopkeeper put his hands up in fear. Told us to take what we wanted. I thought we were just planning on scaring him a bit, but one of the lads lost it. His name was Carl. He's the only one of them I remember. The shopkeeper kept screaming and begging for us not to hurt him. Carl just kept telling him to shut up.

I walked around the store to see if anyone else was in there. Last thing we needed was someone calling the Police. Then, there was a whimper and the screaming stopped. I ran over to the counter from the aisle and saw Carl and the others running out. They shouted for me to come with them, and I froze. The shopkeeper was on the floor, not responding, his shirt covered in red. They shouted at me again, but I was still stuck to the spot. Then one of the other lads grabbed my arm and dragged me out.

We ran for three miles. Throwing the duffel bag full of cash between us, running down alleyways and taking shortcuts. When we eventually stopped, we took off our balaclavas. Carl instantly looked for somewhere to ditch the knife. The rest of the lads started to disperse. I stayed with Carl to help him bury the knife. I wasn't comfortable with that though.

I asked Carl why he had to kill the shopkeeper, and Carl put the knife to my throat, telling me questions like that can get me hurt. I didn't mean anything by it, is what I told him. I also told him it didn't sit right with me. Carl kept the knife to my throat for a few seconds and then laughed. Telling me I was always the funny one. I wasn't joking though.

In the heat of the moment, I disarmed Carl and cut his thigh so he couldn't run away. Carl dropped to the floor. I could have shouted for help, but I didn't. I took the law into my own hands instead. I stood over him and, without saying a word, I put the knife into his stomach. Tears welled up in my eyes, rage was the expression on Carl's face. I pulled the knife out and pushed it back in again as hard as I could. The rage on Carl's face disappeared into peacefulness. Carl was dead, and his evil was gone with him.

I saw blue flashes then. Someone from a nearby street must've called the Police. I dropped the knife and gave myself up to the Police. At court, I plead guilty to Carl's murder and the shopkeeper's murder. I felt just as responsible as everyone else who was there. I never gave up the other lads, but one by one they got picked off by Police. They served less time than me, but I deserve every minute."

Eric took a deep breath. Jake was sat there frozen like a statue. Eric was a murderer? Yes, but he did it for a good reason. Through all his mistakes, he came good. Now all he wanted to do was make amends.

Jake looked up at Eric and could see that he was disappointed in himself. He clearly wasn't proud of his actions. Why would he be?

Jake put his hand on Eric's shoulder. A comforting touch.

"You made a mistake. Everyone makes them. It's how we act on those mistakes that defines us as people." Jake said to Eric. This comforted Eric even more.

"That's why I wanted to help you Jake. A few days before we met, I saw you get beat up by one of the gangs. You hadn't done anything. When the guards helped you up, I saw the same look in your eyes as the shopkeeper. Despair. Weakness. Loss. That's why I wanted to help you. I didn't want to see another person go through what that shopkeeper went through." Eric really wanted to make amends. "Now I have said what I needed to say. I've made my peace. I don't want forgiveness; I just want to redeem myself. Hopefully you can redeem my family's name."

Eric got up from the seat opposite Jake, gave him a nod and said a simple word to him which would stick with Jake.

"Goodbye."

Eric walked away, back into the dark hallway which would take him to his cell. Jake knew something felt different. Eric was different when he left. Jake couldn't quite put his finger on it. Either way, Jake had got his story. So, he got to work writing it.

The story took him over a week to write. He worked seven-hour days in the office writing the story. Once he got home, he would have his dinner and then get straight back to writing the story. It needed to be perfect if he wanted the editor to approve it. Jake was always raised with the belief that nothing would come from laziness. So, he worked hard to make sure that he could make the story into a success.

Once it was finally finished, Jake took the story into the editor and handed it over. The editor said that the story Jake had written was the best that he had ever read from a new journalist. Jake was filled with pride. The paper was printed, and the story made the front page. Eager for Eric to read it, Jake took a copy so he could hand it over to him on the next visiting day.

The visiting day came around quickly, and Jake was over the moon. He went into the room and waited patiently for Eric. He waited. And waited. And waited. Eric never came out. Jake went over to the warden and asked if he could pass the newspaper to Eric, however, the warden's facial expression changed.

"You must be Jake," The warden said with a lump in his throat, "I'm sorry to tell you, Eric died a few days ago."

Jake's world stopped. He was crushed. His best friend. His only friend. His brother. Dead. Gone forever.

"How?" Jake asked, struggling to fight back the tears. That was the only word he could bring himself to say.

"Suicide. He left a note saying that it was his time and that he had made his peace. He wanted to thank you for helping to redeem him and for seeing the good in him." The warden's response was firm but caring at the same time. He could see just how distraught Jake was. Without saying another word, Jake turned around and left. Jake blamed himself for Eric's death. He wanted to help his friend more than tell a story.

Jake didn't go to the funeral. He couldn't bare to say goodbye. He took some time away from work. When he returned, the support he received from his co-workers was beyond what he could imagine. Everyone was moved by the story. They connected with Eric, and so they mourned him with Jake. Jake really did redeem Eric. Eric could rest peacefully knowing that people no longer saw him as the monster that the world had painted him to be. Life goes on, but not for Eric.

Not much else happened to Jake for a while. He got promoted at work and found himself working on the new and big stories. Every story he wrote, he wrote with the same passion which he used in his story about Eric. Jake felt lonely though. He hadn't got any friends, as he struggled to let anyone in for fear of being bullied or losing them like he did Eric. That was until Jake's mother convinced him to try speed dating.

Jake went to speed dating a few times and couldn't see anything working. He promised himself that the next session he went to would be the last one. He sat at the table and waited for someone to sit down. For a while, nobody came over to his table. Just as he went to gather his things and stand up, the chair opposite moved back, and someone took a seat.

Jake looked up and couldn't believe his eyes. A beautiful woman sat opposite him. Long, flowing, blonde hair which faded into brown near to the roots. She clearly dyed it. Blue eyes, cherry red lipstick-covered lips. She had a slim figure covered by an exquisite green dress and was sporting a nametag which read 'JANE.'

Jake was stunned. Surely she had sat at the wrong table?

"Hi Jake, I'm Jane." These were the first words out of his mouth, not realising he had completely fumbled his sentence. Jane giggled.

"Hi Jane, I'm Jake." She replied, making humour out of his comment. The two sat and talked for hours and hours. They had to be ushered out of the room in the end as they stopped way beyond the time they were allocated. Neither of them believed in love at first sight. Yet, they found themselves falling in love. Whatever this was, it was special.

For the next few months, they continued seeing each other. Jake introduced Jane to his family, and Jane introduced Jake to hers. Jane became Jake's rock and Jake became Jane's. On the Christmas of the year two thousand and ten, two years after they met, Jake got down on one knee in front of the incredibly well-decorated Christmas tree.

"Will you marry me?" Jake asked, his arms and legs trembling in anticipation.

"YES!" Jane exclaimed as she jumped up and down in excitement.

Their wedding was a year later. The perfect day and a beautiful ceremony. Jake wore a grey checkered suit whilst Jane wore the classic white dress. They joined together at the altar. They shared their vows. To always be by each other's side. To love, and to hold, for the rest of their lives. To care, to cherish, forever. Until death do them apart.

Once the after-party had finished, the newly-wed couple headed straight home, grabbed their suitcases and took off on their honeymoon. Seven magnificent days in Cyprus. They come home and then begun their new life as a married couple.

Throughout their marriage, they hit various obstacles and for some months found themselves arguing more than showing their love for each other. They made it work though and kept at it.

The biggest argument was around the decision to have children. Jane wanted children but Jake was unable to give children to Jane. They considered adopting but both agreed that it wouldn't be the same. This caused a rift in their relationship which, over time, would continue to grow. Jane would blame

Jake for her not being able to have a child and would make Jake feel awful about it.

Skipping ahead to the year two thousand and seventeen, seven years after the wedding, Jane and Jake were still married. Whether they were truly still happy together was the question, but they tried to make it work. It was more Jake putting in the effort at this point. Jane had seemingly given up on the relationship.

By this time, Jake was thirty-five years old, and Jane was thirty-three. Jane hadn't changed much from when Jake first set eyes on her, but Jake had changed. Jake was bald now with a full beard which was about grade five or six in length. It was well treated. Jake wanted to show that he looked after himself. He was athletic, exercising three times a week. He would run thirty minutes to the gym, lift weights for two hours, and would then run thirty minutes to get home. He dressed well. On his days off he would wear polo shirts and slim-fitting jeans with nice shoes.

At work, he would always wear a suit. He didn't usually wear the blazer, but always wore a waistcoat with a button-up shirt and smart trousers to match the colour of the suit.

Jake was not the timid boy he once was. Since what happened with Eric and meeting his wife Jane, Jake became more and more confident. He would often talk with people in the office and even made friends with some of them. Jake was still working in journalism, for the same outlet that gave him his first big opportunity. Jake worked hard and worked lots of overtime to keep a roof over his and Jane's head.

Jake's day consisted of the same itinerary; wake up at seven o'clock, have a shower and breakfast, drive to work in his Volkswagen Golf GTI which he had proudly earned through hard work, get into work and make the first round of drinks, and sit down ready to start his day.

Little did he know how different today would be.

At half past nine in the morning, deep footsteps could be heard coming up the stairs. Whether it was because the stairs were hollow, or whether the person was heavy-footed, was unknown to Jake at the time. It sounded as if a Tyrannosaurus Rex was making its way up the stairs. The boss come out of the office as Jake spun his chair around to see who was coming up the stairs. Maybe it was just Luke from the accounting department. He was heavy-footed. When Jake fully turned around, he could not believe his eyes.

A stocky man, about six feet in height, stood firm at the top of the stairs. He wasn't fat but he definitely wasn't toned either. He was somewhere in the middle. He had short hair, combed over to his right side. A scruffy beard accompanied the black, square-framed glasses sitting over his eyes. He had his sleeves rolled up, showing off his tattoos. He had turned up in plain, cheap clothes, which were slightly creased. His shirt was untucked, and clearly, he didn't care about his appearance.

The boss went and stood next to the man as Jake

looked on in despair. He knew exactly who this was, but he didn't want to believe it.

"Everyone, this is Reece Stephenson," The boss exclaimed to the team, "Let's give him a warm welcome."

Everyone clapped Reece as he smiled and waved. Everyone except Jake. Jake thought that his nightmare was over. He was wrong. It was just starting.

3 REUNITED, BUT NOT UNITED

"Let me show you to where you'll be working." The boss said as he put his arm around Reece and started directing him. By this time the applause had faded, and everyone was getting back to their work. Jake watched in horror as the seat Reece was guided to was the empty desk next to his own.

"This is Jake. He will be your mentor for the next few weeks. Just follow his lead and I'm sure you'll be fine. You're in capable hands." The boss said to Reece as he placed his bag down and sat in the available seat next to Jake.

"Isn't there anyone else he can work under?" Jake exclaimed, panic-stricken by the thought of having to work with the person who once put him through so much. "I have so much work on, and I don't think I could do a good job."

The boss looked at Jake in a puzzled manner. Jake had never questioned his decisions before. This was a first. Then, after a brief moment of silence, a smile formed on his boss' face.

"I see Jake, you have no need to worry. I'm sure you'll do just fine." The boss said with a polite smile as he turned around to walk back into his office. He had no idea of the history between the pair. He didn't even know that Jake had been to prison, let alone that Reece was the reason for his time there. Jake continued to panic. He looked back at his desk and then over at Reece. Reece looked back and gave him an innocent smile, trying to be friendly. Jake wasn't buying it. Jake rolled his eyes, got up from his desk and started to walk to the boss' office. Then, he turned around and walked back to his desk. He looked at Reece whilst he picked up his phone, car keys, house keys and wallet. He also locked his computer. He wanted Reece to know that there was no trust between them. It was clear that Jake wanted nothing to do with Reece at all. Jake stormed off, going into the office with his boss and shutting the door behind him. Jake also closed the blinds covering the one window where everyone in the main office could see into the small office.

"I can't work with him." Jake said sternly. He wanted to get the point across to his boss immediately.

"Jake. I understand you've got a lot on, but I know you'll do an excellent job at showing Reece the ropes.

If I didn't have faith in you, I wouldn't have picked you for this task." The boss replied, trying to reassure Jake. It was quite clear though that Jake was set in his mind. Jake paced up and down the office a couple of times, scratching his nose. This is something he does when faced with an awkward situation or under great stress.

"You don't understand. I know him. I cannot work with him." Jake replied to his boss, trying to get the point across without being forthcoming about details. Who knows what Reece could tell him?

"Well, if you know each other then that means you'll be able to get acquainted quicker," The boss replied, standing his ground, "My decision isn't changing Jake. You've got this."

Jake's boss winked at him, and then went into a conference meeting online. Jake walked back into the main office, and everyone resumed working as if they hadn't been trying to listen. The journalists there were always so nosey. Jake didn't say anything. He grabbed his notebook, his pen, and his bag. He swung his bag over his shoulder, without even acknowledging Reece's presence. Reece went to speak, but before he could, Jake had started to walk away.

"Where are you going?" Stacey asked Jake. She was the gossiper of the office, so she hated it when she wasn't in the loop of what was going on.

"Out." Jake's response was short and abrupt. He couldn't be bothered with anything or anyone. Jake got into his car and drove out of the car park. Perks of being a journalist, Jake could come and go as he pleased as long as he got the stories in on time.

Jake drove away calmly to start with. He tried to think over what he could do, and what options he had. He did his best thinking when he was driving. He loved his car and he loved to drive. So that's exactly what he did. Jake drove to an old forest area with tight lanes where he could be at one with his car. He pulled out of the junction and put his foot to the floor.

Thirty miles per hour.

Forty miles per hour.

Fifty miles per hour.

Jake stopped looking at the speedometer and kept his focus on the country road ahead of him. It was a straight road, with only a few junctions. The safest place for him to feel alive. Jake looked down at the speedometer again.

Eighty-five miles per hour.

Ninety miles per hour.

One last push. That was all he needed.

One hundred miles per hour.

As soon as he hit one hundred, he came off the throttle, coasting back down and watching his miles per gallon go back up rather than down. That was all he needed to feel alive. Get his heart racing and get the blood pumping. Jake started to think of what he could do or how he could resolve his dilemma.

Jake had a few options. Option one was that he could tell his boss the truth but leave out the part about going to prison. Option two was that he could quit his job and find somewhere else to work. Option three was that he could just suck it up and get on with his job and accept this as his new reality.

He tried calling Jane, but he couldn't get a signal in the area. He pulled up in a layby and stopped to think. He kept the engine running but had his head in his hands. He still couldn't believe that nineteen years after he left school. Nineteen years after he went to prison. Reece was back.

Jake had tried to suppress and hide that part of his life. It became evident that all the horrifying memories that he had put locks and chains on were about to break out. Jake tried to call Jane again. Still no signal. Jake sat in the layby for an hour trying to think of what to do. He decided that he needed to tell his boss the truth. Well, most of it. Jake put his indicator on, checked his path was clear and pulled out of the layby onto the road. From there, he took a nice relaxing drive back to the office. He did have to stop for petrol on the way back, as he used a lot of it in that drive.

Jake pulled back onto the car park and sat in his car for a few minutes. He rehearsed his lines in the mirror of his car. Looking at himself.

"I can't work with him." Jake repeatedly said in the mirror. He said this about three or four times. Each time in a different tone, trying to find one that was equally respectful but firm at the same time. He didn't want to work with Reece, but he didn't want to lose his job either.

Jake walked back into the office and a dull silence followed him in. The office fell quiet. All that could be heard were the sound of Jake's footsteps which followed behind him. Reece turned around in his chair and looked over at Jake.

"Hi Jake." Reece said nervously. Jake didn't even acknowledge Reece. His expression didn't change. He didn't huff. It was like Reece was completely invisible. Jake put his bag on his chair and knocked on his boss' office door.

"Come in." The boss shouted. Jake opened the door, walked in, and shut it behind him. "Where have you been?"

"I had to pop out. I need to talk to you about the Reece situation." Jake said to his boss. The boss looked back at him with sympathy.

"I wish you'd have told me Jake, I completely understand." Jake was puzzled. Then panic set in. 'What has Reece said?' 'Has he told him about me going to prison?' Thoughts rapidly filled Jake's head, as well as panic.

"You do?" Jake replied. The only response he could think of.

"Yes. Reece told me about your past." The boss replied. Jake started panicking. Was he making reference to Jake's prison sentence?

"It was a long time ago." Jake replied, scratching his nose again. His nerves were taking over.

"That doesn't excuse what he put you through. I

mean bullying? It's disgusting. If I'd have known before, believe me, he would be straight out the front door." The boss replied. Jake was relieved. Perhaps Reece hadn't mentioned the part about Jake going to prison. Maybe Jake could keep his secret for a while longer.

"I know," Jake said in response, "Some of the things he used to do to me were inhumane. That's why I can't work with him."

Jake's boss looked over at him, still holding that same sympathy in his eyes which he had when Jake entered the office to have this discussion.

"Reece has said he wants to apologise though. It might be worth hearing him out." Jake's boss replied. Jake couldn't believe what he was hearing. Hear him out? Seriously?

Jake shook his head. "The damage was done a long time ago. Nothing can heal that. I don't care how sorry he is, I don't want to hear his apology and I don't want to work with him."

The room fell silent. The boss looked down. Jake took a moment to evaluate the situation. He realised he had the opportunity to be the bigger person here.

"I won't tutor him. But I will be civil with him." Jake said, much to the surprise of his boss. "That's it though. Just civil for the sake of this company."

His boss smiled. He knew Jake was a strong person, especially with what happened after Eric passed away. They had worked together that long that they considered each other to be friends.

"Very well," The boss said, "I will try and find him another mentor. In the meantime, if he has any questions, answer them for him. You don't have to be friendly with him. Just do what's best for the paper."

Jake could agree to this. It meant he would have to bite his tongue every five minutes, but these were terms that he could get behind. Jake walked back to his desk and sat down. Reece was still sat next to him, quietly twiddling his thumbs in awkwardness. He wanted to speak to Jake. He genuinely wanted to apologise, but even he knew that now wasn't the time to do that. He wanted to let Jake calm down first.

Jake carried on with the rest of his day, with Reece sitting next to him trying to make small talk where he could. At the end of the day, Jake collected his belongings and walked outside. There he saw a car. A black Ford Fiesta with the registration plate RC57 SON. 'Reece Stephenson' Jake thought to himself. Jake shook his head, still in disbelief, and continued walking towards his car.

Jake usually enjoyed his drive home from work. It was his chance to unwind. Instead, he spent the whole time thinking about how he was going to move forward with Reece sat next to him in the office.

When Jake got home, Jane was cooking dinner for them both.

"How was your day sweetie?" That was Jane's little pet name for Jake when she was in one of her good moods.

"Unbelievable. We had a new starter. Some twat I

know from school started today as a newbie." Jake told Jane.

"Well, it's strange how you've become reunited. What are the chances?" Jane replied to Jake.

"Reunited, but not united. The brat used to bully me in school." Jake responded, sitting down at the table to enjoy his cup of tea which Jane had just made for him, "And worst of all, I've been asked to train him."

Jane looked on at Jake in sympathy. The same sympathetic look that his boss looked at him with. She knew Jake had been bullied but didn't know to what extent. She definitely didn't know about his prison sentence. He'd done his best to conceal that from her and put it in the past.

"He's told the boss that he's sorry and he keeps trying to make conversation with me," Jake said to Jane as she sat at the other end of the small table in the kitchen, "But I'm not buying it."

"Are you going to be tutoring him?" Jane asked Jake, "I mean, if you've got to work with him anyways, you might as well."

Jake looked over at Jane as if she had gone mad. She didn't know all that Reece and his group had put Jake through though. She was just innocent to the whole matter and wanted to see the best in people.

"Why did you think that?" Jake asked Jane, wanting to know the reason behind her baffling suggestion.

"If you tutor him, you can see if he actually wants

to make amends and see if he actually is sorry." Jane said to Jake, stretching out her hand across the table and taking a hold of his. "If he isn't, you can always botch his training and then he won't be there much longer."

Jake laughed and Jane shared a giggle too. Maybe her baffling idea wasn't so baffling after all. Maybe she was onto something. This was Jake's chance to listen and, for once, be the bigger man. If Jake could tutor Reece, he could find out his true intentions. He still didn't trust Reece but tutoring him wasn't such a bad idea after all.

Jake slept on it. Not literally. He slept on the thought of it. The next morning, he woke up and followed the same itinerary as the days before Reece came back into his life.

On Jake's drive into work, just before he got to the office, a black Fiesta pulled out of the car park of a local off licence. The Fiesta pulled onto the road just ahead of Jake. He knew instantly that it was Reece because of the registration plate. Jake followed Reece into the office car park. The pair of them got out of their cars at similar times. Jake parked in a corner spot to avoid his car getting bumped, whereas Reece parked close to the door.

As he walked to the door, rather than ignoring Reece, Jake swallowed his pride and spoke one simple word. One word which would change everything.

"Hello." That was it. That was the word that Jake said to Reece. Reece was as shocked as Jake was.

Reece followed Jake in, who held the door open for him.

Reece sat at his desk, and Jake put his bag down and went straight into the boss' office. He kept his keys and valuables with him though. Just because he said 'hello' to Reece didn't mean that he could trust him yet. Jake walked into the office and shut the door.

"Morning Boss." Jake said, opening the conversation.

"Morning Jake," The boss responded, "Have you gave any more thought to the proposal?"

Jake nodded his head. "I'll mentor him, and I'll be civil with him, on one condition."

The boss nodded in both shock and understanding. He was hoping that Jake wasn't going to ask for extra pay as the company couldn't afford another set of pay rises so soon after the ones three months prior.

"What is it?" The boss answered.

"I want to use the conference room for an hour. Me and Reece are going to talk and go through everything that happened. I want Reece to listen to me, and I want him to really understand how he made me feel." Jake demanded. Not in a rude way, but in a polite way. Polite enough that the point he was trying to make would get through.

"If that's what it takes, then yes that's fine. I'll talk to Reece now." The boss said to Jake. Jake smiled and turned around, walking to the door. As he got to the door, the boss had one more thing to say. Jake looked back.

"Jake, I really appreciate you being so mature about this. It takes a lot for someone to do what you're doing, and I admire you for it." The boss told Jake. Jake smiled.

"Thank you, boss." He said gratefully. Jake left the office and went and sat back in his seat. The boss called Reece in and relayed what Jake had said. Reece was in the office with the boss for about ten minutes. The blind was shut, so Jake couldn't tell what was being said.

Reece came back out of the office and sat down next to Jake. He moved slightly over towards Jake who continued to stare into the deep abyss of his computer screen.

"Whenever you're ready to talk, let me know." Reece said to Jake. This lifted a weight off Jake's shoulders. He knew that Reece had agreed to the terms of Jake training him. Maybe Reece had changed. The Reece from high school would never have entertained speaking to Jake, let alone apologise for bullying him.

"Shall we talk now?" Jake asked as he looked up at Reece. Reece nodded at Jake and got up first. Jake showed Reece to the conference room and shut the door behind them both. Jake went over to the water cooler and got two plastic cups, filling them with water. He placed one in front of where Reece had sat and then put two seats between himself and Reece but sat at the same side of the table that Reece did.

The two sat in silence for a moment. Jake was thinking of what to say first. He didn't think it would actually come to this, so he had no plan for what he intended to say. All he knew was that it needed to come from the heart to get through to Reece.

"Where do I start? I've got loads of questions and loads of feelings which I need to get off my chest." Jake opened with that. Reece looked down. Then back up and nodded at Jake.

"I understand. Take your time." Reece responded. A shock to Jake but something which reassured him. Jake took a moment and then continued.

"Well firstly, I want you to know how you all made me feel." Jake said to Reece, looking him in the eye. Reece nodded before putting his head down again in shame.

"Every single day you and the others targeted me. Made me feel worthless. Made me hate every waking moment of my life. People say school is supposed to be the best days of your life, but you took those good days away from me. Not once did I react to you. Not once did I retaliate. I ran away, I turned the other cheek, I never told anyone. Not even my parents. I let you do it because I thought one day, you would stop. You never did. Punch after punch, kick after kick, it got worse each time. The one day I did react, I'm the one who gets punished for it. I was hoping you'd come through with some honesty, but no, you couldn't even bring yourself to do that. You ruined my life. Even now, I struggle with my confidence. I struggle talking to people. I'm constantly anxious. I'm paranoid. I'm always looking over my shoulder. These are all traits which I've had from your actions." Jake stopped and took a deep breath.

Emotions were running high for him. He'd never had the strength to confront his school bully. He looked away from Reece and down at the floor. When he looked back up, Reece still had his head down in shame.

Jake had a new, strange, feeling come over him. A sense of power. He had finally stood up for himself against his childhood bully without having to use violence.

Both of them were speechless for a moment. Then Reece said something which took Jake by complete surprise.

"I'm sorry," Those two words meant the world to Jake, "I had no idea how we made you feel."

Jake was stunned. He knew Reece wanted to apologise but he never expected him to actually do it. Jake took a sip of his water, trying to digest what he had just heard.

"I just need to know one thing," Jake responded, putting his plastic cup on the table, "Why?"

Reece looked up, tears welling up in his eyes, "I don't know. Maybe it was jealousy. Maybe we were just evil. I know it's not good enough, but I can't give you an honest answer."

"So you did it just because you felt like it?" Jake

replied, trying to prompt a better answer out of Reece. He wasn't happy with the one he'd just had off him.

"That's the best way of describing it. I want you to know, it was never anything personal-" Reece was cut short by Jake.

"Well it felt personal!" Jake snapped back at Reece as he launched up from his chair, causing it to rock backwards and hit the floor. He looked Reece straight in the eyes. Reece was fighting back tears. At that moment, Jake realised that Reece was actually sorry. He was telling the truth and he genuinely regretted what he put Jake through. All those years gone by, and Jake finally got what he wanted. Reece apologising. Jake had won.

The pair didn't say anything for a while. Jake bent down and picked up the chair. He sat down and waited for a moment, then, Jake opened his mouth again.

"Whilst I was in prison, I made a friend. Eric. He was a fantastic lad. Twice the person any of us could think of being. He was in there for murder. He owned up to his mistakes and was doing his time." Jake said to Reece. Reece looked up, trying to figure out what point Jake was making.

"He taught me that even the worst of actions are redeemable," Jake stretched his hand out, prompting Reece to shake it, "I may not be able to forgive you easily, but I can try my hardest to."

Reece shook Jake's hand. This was the first step on

a long road for the pair of them. Reece admired Jake from this point on. Jake's actions spoke louder than his words and Reece truly respected that. He knew it would take time, but Reece hoped that Jake could forgive him. Reece even hoped that one day the two may actually be friends. It would be a long road but one that Reece was willing to walk.

4 TENSIONS

After their meeting, the two started working together. Jake started to show Reece the ropes of journalism but remained distant to him. Despite their heartfelt conversation, Jake was keeping Reece at an arm's length. He needed to be civil with him for the sake of their job. At the same time, he couldn't trust him.

Reece was just happy that the two of them were getting along and he could get on with learning the role. He knew that there was trust issues there. He could understand why. He had spent over three years making Jake's life a waking nightmare, so he knew that would have something to do with it. He never asked, he never passed a comment, and he accepted that it was going to be like that for a while. That didn't stop Reece from trying to befriend Jake, despite there clearly being tensions between them.

These tensions became clear after just a few days of them working together. One day, Jake and Reece went out to someone's house to get some details from them on a potential story. Jake was to take the lead in speaking to the person, while Reece's role was to sit back and observe. There had been some robberies in the local area, and the Police hadn't got the resources or the capability to deal with it. Naturally, the victim of one of the robberies turned to the media. This was where Jake and Reece came in.

They took Jake's car. Reece's car was old and filthy. It wouldn't look good if that's what they turned up in. Jake took pride in his car, so he offered to drive. He didn't tell Reece that was the reason, he just said he liked driving. It didn't phase Reece either way, his role was just to follow Jake. So, he did.

Jake looked for the number of the house. Number sixty-one. He pulled up outside the house, parked half on the kerb and half on the road, making sure to leave enough room for pedestrians so that no-one hit his wing mirror. It had happened to him once before and he didn't fancy letting it happen again.

The pair got out of the car and Reece slammed the car door a bit too hard. It was on accident, and he instantly apologised, but Jake just tutted and rolled his eyes. Reece didn't say anything. He just put it down to their more than complicated history.

The front lawn was secured by a gate, which Jake opened and left open for Reece to walk through. The lawn was well maintained, with plenty of plants which were looked after and a few lawn ornaments. Just from looking and using his experience, Jake could instantly figure one thing out.

"I'm putting money on this person being retired. Be prepared to see some flower wallpaper in the house." Jake whispered to Reece.

"What makes you say that?" Reece replied with a smirk on his face. He was puzzled by Jake's comment.

"Instinct," Jake replied with confidence in his voice, "Trust me."

Reece found it ironic that Jake told him to trust him. Given that Jake didn't trust Reece, he just found the comment to be amusing. He kept this to himself though. The smallest of comments could set Jake off. He stood back as he watched Jake knock on the door. About twenty seconds passed and the two remained standing there.

"Maybe try knocking again." Reece suggested to Jake. Jake turned around and looked at Reece.

"Give them a minute, if they're elderly it'll take them a while to get to the door." Jake replied to Reece. Another ten seconds passed, and the door started to unlock. Jake looked back at Reece and smiled, knowing his instincts were correct. Reece was somewhat impressed.

The door partially opened. A frail, white-haired, elderly lady looked through the opening. She was only small, clearly not very mobile either. She kept the safety latch on as she peeped out, not knowing who was on the other side.

"Can I help you?" The lady asked.

"My names Jake, and this is my colleague Reece, we're from the local paper. You called us to tell us you had a story about something which had happened to you?" Jake told the lady in a calm, softly spoken voice. He could see the lady was shaken up by what had happened to her, so he was ready to be as patient as he needed to be.

"Do you have any ID?" The elderly lady asked Jake. Jake got his staff ID card out which he used to get in and out of the office. It was blue and had his name and picture on it.

"Excuse the photo, it's an old one." Jake said this to put the elderly lady at ease. Jake lowered his card and the lady looked over at Reece, who was standing with his hands in his pockets looking at the plants. Jake looked back at Reece and widened his eyes to signal to him. Reece looked back and was puzzled. He clearly hadn't been listening.

"Reece, where's your ID?" Jake asked Reece firmly. He couldn't believe Reece's attitude.

"Right, sorry." Reece replied, reaching into his pocket, and pulling out his brand-new ID card given to him on his first day. The lady shut the door and undid the latch to let them in.

"For that, you can offer to make the drinks." Jake said to Reece, clearly annoyed at his ignorance. Reece rolled his eyes as Jake turned back around. The lady then opened the door and the two walked in. She showed them to the living room where the pair sat down on a cream-coloured sofa. Jake looked over at Reece who took a second to realise. He stood back up and offered to make the drinks.

"Oh, how sweet. I'll have a tea with two sugars please, plenty of milk," The lady responded, delighted at the prospect of not having to make the drinks for a change, "Kitchen is just through the dining room, on the right. Mugs are in the second cupboard on the left."

"Tea, no sugar, please. Just a dash of milk." Jake replied to Reece as he looked over to see if Jake wanted anything to drink. Reece nodded and turned around, opening the door to the dining room. He shut the door behind him and that's when he saw it. Right there on the dining room wall. Flower wallpaper. Surely Jake had been here before. Surely his instincts weren't that good? Reece walked into the kitchen, shaking his head but smiling in disbelief. Meanwhile, Jake got started on the questions.

"So, let's start with your name." Jake said, smiling and taking his notepad out of his rear trouser pocket. In all his years of journalism, he always kept it in the exact same place. He usually misplaced things, but not his notepad.

"Harriet Armstrong." The lady said in response to Jake who made a note in his notepad.

"And unfortunately, I do have to ask your age as well. Should I put down twenty-one?" Jake asked in a joking manner. He wanted to make her feel as comfortable as possible. Harriet laughed.

"Stop it, I'm eighty-one." She replied with a smile on her face. Jake smiled back, he was happy to be making her comfortable.

"So, what date did the robbery happen?" Jake replied. Harriet put her finger up to indicate that she would be one moment and made her way over to her diary which was on the table near the living room window. As she flicked through the dates, Reece came back into the room with three mugs. One for Harriet, one for Jake, and one for himself.

"I love your wallpaper." Reece said to Harriet as he looked over at Jake and smiled. Jake smiled back.

"Thank you, I've had it up for years." Harriet responded as she flicked through her diary.

"Mrs Armstrong is just checking the dates for us of when the incident happened." Jake informed Reece. He mainly said this to tell Reece what her name was without making it obvious to Harriet. Reece nodded and took note in this notepad, which he kept in his back pocket the same as Jake.

"It was Thursday 23rd February," Harriet told Jake and Reece, pointing at her diary and showing Jake, "It would have been around two o'clock in the afternoon because I was coming back from the bank in town."

Jake proceeded to make notes and ask Harriet questions to get enough details to write the story. Reece sat back and listened, making a few notes but not many. Jake noticed this but didn't see it to be the appropriate time to pass a comment to Reece. They finished their drinks and a few biscuits that Harriet had been and got for them. Digestives to be exact. They then said their goodbyes and off they went.

They walked back down the path and Jake shut the gate behind them. He unlocked the car and they both got in. Jake sat silent for a moment.

"That went well." Reece said, trying to fill the silence.

"Did it?" Jake asked, looking over at Reece, "I didn't see you make any notes."

Reece pointed to his head, "It's all up here, don't worry."

"If that's the case, what was the name of the street where it happened on?" Jake asked Reece, putting him on the spot.

"Easy, Rosendale Drive. Just outside Kolodynski's garage." Reece responded with confidence, he was correct after all.

Jake nodded, "Fair enough. I'm surprised given your ignorance at the start."

"Ignorance?" Reece looked back at Jake in confusion. What had he done this time?

"When Harriet asked for your ID card earlier and you were staring at her plants?" Jake clarified, clearly annoyed, "You were miles away."

"Right, sorry. Just got a lot on my mind." Reece said in response.

"Well in this job, you need to listen as much as possible. It's not like when we were in school, you're telling people's stories here. They're trusting you to tell them right. How can you do that if you're too busy getting distracted by plants?" Jake replied, venting his frustration at Reece.

"Sorry, lesson learned." Reece replied, putting his head down. Jake looked away from Reece and started the car.

"You made a good cup of tea though, I'll give you that." Jake told Reece, trying to lighten the mood as he released the handbrake and pulled away. He was still getting used to the whole 'go be a mentor to the kid who used to bully you' thing. Reece smiled at him, as Jake drove them both back to the office.

They got back to the office just after lunchtime, which was usually around one o'clock in the afternoon. Jake went and heated up leftovers from last night's dinner. Lasagne. He put a dash of salt over it and went back to his desk. Reece came and sat next to him and the two got to work on typing their notes up on their separate computers. This was going to be Jake's article, and Reece was going to shadow him. This was the last time Reece would shadow Jake before writing his own article. Reece felt he wasn't ready, but Jake knew he was.

Before they knew it, five o'clock had rolled around and it was time for them to head off home. The article was nearly finished, so they could finish it tomorrow and get it submitted before the end of the week. Reece had worked hard today, and Jake had noticed. As they packed up their bags, Jake remembered that he was going to be on his own tonight – Jane was going out with the girls.

It had stuck in Jake's head what Reece had said about having a lot on his mind. Whilst he was still trying to forgive him for their past, Jake couldn't help but feel like he had to be supportive. As a colleague of course. He didn't want to refer to him as a friend just yet.

"Do you fancy getting a pint?" Jake asked Reece. Reece looked over at him and smiled.

"Sure, if you can keep up." Reece replied, trying to make a joke out of the situation. He was surprised Jake had asked him to go out given how he was with him earlier.

"I know a good bar not too far from my place if you want to go there?" Jake asked, picking up his bag and slinging it over his right shoulder.

Reece nodded, "I'll follow you there."

They parked up at Jake's house. Jake parked on the drive and Reece parked on the road. They then took a short walk to the local pub. When they got in, it was busier than Reece expected. Jake knew what it would be like. After all, this wasn't just any pub, this was Chadwick's Tavern. The best pub in the area. Jake bought two beers and a packet of pork scratchings for them to share between them. The two sat down and got to talking.

"So, you said earlier you'd got a lot on your mind," Jake said, prompting Reece to look up from his gorgeous golden-coloured pint, "What's going on?"

"It's nothing, don't worry. Too much to get into."

Reece responded. Jake didn't want to pry at this stage, so he accepted that Reece didn't want to talk and moved on. The two continued to drink and finished their individual pints.

Reece went straight up to the bar and bought two more pints for them. They clanged their glasses together and carried on drinking. Once those beers were finished, Reece bought another two.

And another two.

And another two.

Jake was starting to feel a bit tipsy, Reece meanwhile was like a beer-drinking machine. 'Was he intolerant to alcohol?'

Jake couldn't stomach another pint, so he got up to get some more drinks so he could have a break from all the alcohol. Jake had an orange and passionfruit drink, whilst Reece had yet another pint. He was starting to slur his words slightly, but Jake could still understand what Reece was saying. At least, he thought he could.

"Jacob!" Reece randomly exclaimed, "Thank you so, so, so much for asking me to this place. It's wonderful!"

Jake laughed. Only his mom called him Jacob, and that was when he was in trouble. He couldn't help but find Reece's drunken state amusing.

"Don't worry about it, I just wanted to make sure you were okay. You seemed a bit off earlier." Jake told Reece. Reece swayed his head a bit and then leaned forward.

"You know what it is Jacob?" Reece whispered to Jake, putting his hand on his shoulder. Jake tried to hold in his laugh as he could sense Reece was about to say something which might be important.

"I just love beer!" Reece shouted, raising both hands in the air and spilling a bit of beer out of his glass. Maybe it wasn't going to be anything important. He could already tell Reece liked his beer by the rate in which he was drinking them. Jake had never seen anything like it. Reece finished his pint and put his glass on his head.

"You know what we need now?" Reece asked Jake, more as a set-up for a statement rather than a genuine question.

"An ambulance?" Jake responded, trying to be witty. Reece gave him a confused look.

"No silly," Reece stood up at speed and raised his arms again, "JAMMYBUCAS!"

'What is a Jammybuca?' Jake thought to himself. Was it a new drink that he hadn't heard about? Then it hit him. He meant Sambucas.

"I think you've had enough." Jake said, laughing at Reece's behaviour.

"You're right." Reece said back as he sat down again. Jake stood up and picked up his coat.

"Come on, you can kip on my sofa," Jake said, nodding at Reece to stand back up, "We better get you somewhere that doesn't have alcohol."

Reece laughed hysterically. A proper drunken laugh. He stood up, put his coat on, and followed

Jake out of the pub. The two walked back home, Jake got in and directed Reece to the living room. Jane was waiting up for Jake. She opened the kitchen door and stood with her arms folded.

"Ooooo you're in the shit. You're in the shit." Reece shouted, pointing at Jake and giggling like a child. Jake told him to shush.

"Where have you been?" Jane asked Jake, clearly unimpressed by his antics. Jake went to answer but Reece put his hand in front of Jake.

"Don't worry, I've got this." Reece whispered to Jake, slurring his words. This was not a good sign for either of them. Jake braced himself that he would be sleeping in the living room as well.

"The PUB!" Reece shouted back, pointing at Jane, "By the way you're gorgeous."

Jane tutted and rolled her eyes.

"Jane, this is Reece. Reece, this is Jane. My wife." Jake introduced them both to each other. Not that Jane would forget Reece.

"Hello. Jane my wife," Reece said to Jane before turning to Jake, "Why isn't her last name Lawson?"

Jane laughed and went up the stairs. Reece was quite funny in his drunken state.

"Is it German? No, wait, it's French. Italian? Scouse?" Reece was listing off possible nationalities for where Jane's new surname had come from. Although Jake couldn't quite remember Scouse being a nationality.

"Her last name is Lawson. She's my wife." Jake

explained quietly, conscious that Jane would be getting ready to go to bed.

Reece stood still and pulled a face which shown that he understood. He tapped Jake on the shoulder and stuck his thumb up whilst giving the strangest wink that Jake had ever seen a person do. Reece seemed to be impressed by Jane. Jake sat him down on the sofa and got him a blanket and a pillow.

"Reece, what did you do after we left school?" Jake asked, sitting down on the seat next to the sofa Reece was lying on.

"Not much really. Joined the army and got shot at. Shot back. Got married. Had a kid. Got divorced. Wife took my son," Reece replied as if it was completely normal, "Then the house. Then my money for CSA."

Jake was speechless. No wonder Reece had been feeling down. He had quite literally been through the wars.

"Reece, that's horrible. I'm so sorry." Jake replied to Reece, genuinely feeling sorry for him. Reece didn't say anything, he just smiled.

Jake stepped out to sort some water and some paracetamol for Reece for in the morning. By the time he got back into the room, Reece was snoring his head off. Fast asleep.

Jake pulled the blanket up a bit more and turned off the lights. Jake then headed upstairs to go to bed. Poor Reece, he had been through so much. Jake couldn't even begin to imagine what it must have been like for him. He struggled to believe that this was the same person who had caused him all those problems so many years ago. He wanted to keep an eye on Reece for the next few days, so that's what he would plan to do. Jake got into bed next to Jane.

"Nice to see you two getting along." Jane said, rolling over to face Jake in bed. Jake saw her smile and smiled back. He gave her a soft kiss.

"Goodnight." Jake said. Jane said it back. Then they both drifted off to sleep.

5 A FRIENDSHIP BLOSSOMING

Over the next few weeks, Jake and Reece became closer and closer. They never spoke about what Reece mentioned when he had passed out on Jake's sofa after getting drunk. Jake wanted to speak to Reece about it but couldn't find the right time. All Jake knew was that he had to keep an eye on Reece. He was starting to like him. Maybe there was a friendship blossoming after all. The unlikeliest of friends. Jake didn't want to admit it, but he cared about Reece.

Jake taught Reece more about journalism and how to be a good writer. Reece was learning from one of the best and it started to show. After two weeks, he already had an article on the front cover. It shocked Jake but deep down he knew that Reece had the potential, he just needed to show it.

They ended up working on a lot of articles and

pieces together. Each time they would alternate as to who got the credit. The boss knew what they were doing and, whilst he wasn't particularly fond of people working together, he could see they were working well. Plus, he was happy that the two had been able to put their differences aside. The boss never knew Jake to hold a grudge as he had against Reece. He could understand why he did hold that grudge though.

The pair even started to do things together on weekends outside of work. Reece used to play for the local Sunday football league team. It was his local pub's team which was called Fradley's arms. They weren't the best, but they were good enough to be a mid-table side. Reece asked Jake if he wanted to join the team, he remembered that Jake used to try and play football in school. Jake agreed to play and was added to the group.

However, there was a catch.

Jake turned up to his first Sunday match which kicked off at three o'clock in the afternoon. It meant he would miss the car racing, but he could always record it. He just had to make sure he didn't check his phone.

When Jake got there, he saw a few familiar faces. All of which made him uncomfortable. He recognised each of the lads; Ryan Green – who was sporting a new scar on his forehead thanks to his and Jake's last confrontation, Fred King, Olly Foster, and Jason Moore. All the lads from the group who used to bully him in school.

Jake felt really uneasy. However, he gritted his teeth and approached the group.

"Hey." Jake said to Reece, sharing slight glances with the other four guys. He didn't want to make too much eye contact because he didn't know what they would say.

"Hey mate, you remember the guys don't you?" Reece replied. For a second it had slipped his mind that these weren't Jake's friends. They were quite the opposite.

"How could I forget?" Jake stated, clearly showing he was not amused by them being there. There was silence for a moment, then Ryan stepped forwards towards Jake. Jake wanted to step back but he knew he needed to stand his ground. Ryan put his hand out to shake Jake's hand.

"Sorry Jake, from all of us," Ryan told Jake. Jake was shocked, especially after he had put Ryan in hospital. Jake shook Ryan's hand.

"No hard feelings, me and Reece have cleared it up so I don't see why we all can't." Jake said, trying to be the better person. He was right after all, if he could make peace with Reece then why couldn't he make peace with the others?

Ryan nodded and Jake proceeded to shake the hands of all the others in the group. They had a brief catch up before being called over by the manager who was handing out kits.

"What position do you play?" The manager, Paul,

asked Jake.

"Preferably left midfield but I can switch to the right." Jake responded. He expected to start on the subs bench as he'd not been able to make Tuesday's training session.

"Perfect, you're starting on the left then." Paul said as he threw a scrunched-up top to Jake. Clearly still dirty from the last game. Jake was shocked that he was going to be starting until Reece pointed out that their left midfielder had twisted his ankle in training and couldn't play. They had nobody else to fill the position so naturally, Jake was chosen.

Jake gave his top a brush down. It was a light blue colour with a local building company on the front as the sponsor. Not a company he'd ever heard of. He turned the kit around to reveal his number. Number seventeen. Jake smiled. He put the top on and started to join in with the warmup. Heel flicks, high knees, stretches, and a few other usual techniques. They got into a bit of pre-match training and then the manager called them over to go over the tactics with them.

They were playing a four-four-two formation. Simple football. Jake was the left midfielder, Ryan at centre-back, Jason was in central midfield, and Reece was the striker. Fred and Olly were left on the bench. They got into formation and then the whistle blew, signalling the start of the forty-five-minute half.

Jake was panting after a measly ten minutes, realising just how unfit he was. He still gave it his all though. Time passed and Jake was making the odd few passes to teammates.

Thirty minutes passed and the opposition had won a corner. They played it short, however, Ryan managed to get in a good tackle and played the ball to Jason. The counterattack was starting. Jason played it to one of the other guys on the team. Jake started sprinting down the left side of the pitch. Jake called for the ball, which came over the top as a through ball. He was one on one with another defender.

Realising he hadn't got the speed to outrun him, Jake slowed down which gave Reece time to get closer to the box. Jake performed a well-executed stepover, which caught the defender off guard. This gave Jake the space to play the ball through to Reece. Reece hit the ball with as much power as he could. The ball flew past the keeper and went into the net.

Goal!!!

Reece ran straight over to Jake and jumped at him. They all celebrated as other players on the team ran over. They finished their celebrations and got back into formation. They carried on playing.

They ended up winning the game three goals to one. Reece got a second goal whilst the other striker managed to score a goal as well. Their opponents did get a goal in, but it ended up just being a consolation goal.

They all ended up going to the pub afterwards for a drink to celebrate their victory. Jake only stayed for the one pint and then had to get home to Jane. He'd already pushed his luck enough with his lads outing to the pub. He sat at home with Jane and they had a lovely roast beef dinner together.

"How did you get on?" Jane asked Jake, looking over as he was trying to fit a whole roast potato into his mouth in one go. Jake held his finger up, asking for one second whilst he chewed his food.

"We won three one, so yeah it went well." Jake replied eventually having eaten his roast potato. The best part of a roast dinner.

Jane smiled. She was finally happy that Jake had some friends and was getting out a bit more. Whilst she did miss spending as much time with him as possible, she was happy that he was happy.

"A few of the lads from school were there," Jake said, "Some of the ones who used to bully me."

Jane was a bit speechless for a moment until Jake added a bit of clarity which gave Jane some reassurance.

"Don't worry though, we've cleared it up. I'll struggle to forgive them, but I can try to move on." Jake told Jane, reassuring her that everything was okay. He could see she was clearly concerned for him. She remembers the impact that seeing Reece had on him. Jane nodded and her smile returned to her face. The two carried on eating and finished their dinners.

For the next few days, Jake would be at work, but Reece would be off sick. He'd had to make an urgent visit to the hospital where he was kept in overnight. When Reece got back, Jake tried to ask Reece what had happened however, as per usual, Reece was a closed book and would not reveal anything.

Jake continued to bond with Reece and the two became inseparable. However, this started to put a rift between Jane and Jake. Jane started complaining that Jake was spending too much time with Reece. Over the coming weeks, Jane and Jake would argue repeatedly. Jake found himself sleeping on the sofa all too many times. Luckily, he had a games console in the living room so he would just be able to put that on for the nights when he couldn't sleep.

While he was happy to have an evolving friendship with Reece, he was missing the old times with Jane when they wouldn't argue and would sit up giggling through the night. Those times were long gone though, especially with the revelation that Jake couldn't give Jane children. Still, Jake fought for the marriage as much as he could.

The more time he spent on the sofa though, the more time he felt distant from his wife. So, Jake just started to go out with Reece more and more to the pub. While it wasn't a good habit, Jake wasn't one for facing problems. Sure, he faced the issues with Reece head-on, but he did run away first. This was him doing the same thing again. Jake knew this wasn't his smartest move, but he had Reece to talk to and get some advice.

"I just don't know what to do anymore," Jake said, knowing Reece would listen to him, "She used to complain that I didn't get out enough. Now I do go out and she complains that I'm not at home enough.

I'm in a lose-lose situation here."

"Start getting her to come out with you when we all go out," Reece replied, picking up his pint from the sticky pub table, "She might just be feeling left out."

Reece had a valid point. One that Jake hadn't even considered. Maybe part of his and Jane's issues were caused because Jane wasn't invited. Maybe she wanted to be out with Jake when he was going out. It was a long shot. The pub scene had never seemed to be to her liking. Nevertheless, it was worth a try. For all Jake knew, it could work.

"We're all having another get-together soon. Lads night out." Reece told Jake. 'Lads night out' referred to himself, Ryan, Fred, Olly, and Jason getting pints at the Fradley's arms. Their local pub and the pub they all represent in the Sunday football league.

"You could always bring Jane with you." Reece added. The idea was going round and round in Jake's head. Jake caved in and agreed. He'd have to introduce Jane to the other guys anyway at some point. This seemed like the best way to do it.

Jake headed home early that night. Jane was lying across the sofa and was wrapped up in a blanket watching a movie. Some sort of rom-com film. Jake entered the living room and took a seat next to Jane, causing her to have to move her legs. Jake put his hand on her leg.

"I'm sorry I haven't been around much," Jake opened the conversation, "I've just been caught up in actually having a group of friends who actually seem to want me around."

Jane looked over in anger, "So what? I don't want you around. Is that what you're saying?"

"No. I didn't mean it like that," Jake hurried to correct himself, trying not to dig a deeper hole than he already had, "You've been wanting me to get out with friends. Now I'm doing it and you seem to be mad at me."

"I just don't understand how you can go from hating Reece one moment to being his best friend the next moment." Jane fired back at Jake.

"Well, maybe you could come out with us all next time and see what all the fuss is about." Jake replied with a cautious smile. He didn't know how Jane would reply to him. It was the nicest way which he could think of asking. Jane paused to think for a moment before she gave her answer. She could tell this was Jake trying to be nice.

"Sure, if they're happy with me coming. This doesn't mean you're out of the doghouse though." Jane replied, smiling back at Jake. It was a sort of sweet smile that she gave him. This was good enough for Jake. He gave her a kiss on the cheek and took himself to bed. Jane followed not long after.

Maybe, just maybe, he was slowly getting out of the doghouse. That would be something he would have to wait and find out though.

6 RUINED

After their chat, Jake and Jane got back on speaking terms. The get-together wasn't for another week, so Jake decided to spend more time with Jane. He explained it to Reece who understood. Besides Jake wasn't married to Reece so he didn't really have any commitments to seeing him. Jake took Jane out to dinner one night at this fancy steakhouse. He wanted to treat her and apologise for not being around her as much.

Jake loved steak and he knew Jane loved it too. On their first proper date, they went to a steakhouse. It's always expensive for them but worth every penny. Jake ordered a Sirloin which he had cooked to medium rare, whilst Jane ordered a rib-eye which she had cooked well done as she didn't like the blood. Jake had tried to explain that it was protein and not blood, but she still had it cooked well done regardless. At that point, it was roast beef and not steak. That was Jake's point of view on it anyways.

They got back from the steakhouse and cuddled up and watched a film together. They both enjoyed having quality time with each other. A bit of time together seemed to be the cure to their constant bickering.

They decided to book a weekend away for three weeks' time. This was for some time in July towards the start of the month. It gave them something to look forward to and would give them a chance to get away from all the stresses of normal life. The weekend away was in a little cabin which was practically in the middle of nowhere. Perfect for a relaxing time. It had a hot tub, a nice warm fire, and barely any distractions, meaning they would have to pay attention to each other. They had been there before, so they knew it was bound to be good.

The get-together came around quicker than expected. To nobody's surprise, it was at the Fradley's arms. Reece told Jake at work to get there at seven o'clock in the evening, however, he and Jane were there slightly early due to going out for food before. They got to the pub at just after quarter to seven and were waiting on the others.

Reece was the first to turn up at quarter past seven. The rest followed suit and by half past seven everyone had arrived. They all congregated around a long, ten-seater, table in the corner of the pub. Jake was already on his second pint by the time that the last few people had arrived, whilst Jane was still on her first glass of wine. She wasn't a big drinker, so she was taking it slow to avoid getting drunk. Seated around the table were; Jake, Jane, Reece, Ryan, Fred, Jason, and Olly. Jake and Jane sat next to each other with Reece and Olly seated opposite. The others were bunched up in three of the remaining six seats.

Jake started taking his drinking slow as he didn't want to embarrass Jane. They stayed at the table for about an hour before deciding to move over to the pool table where they played doubles. Fred and Olly were on a team together as the pair were practically inseparable, Reece and Ryan made up another team, then it was Jake and Jane which left Jason to float around and play whenever he felt like it. He would jump onto anyone's team for the odd game. For most of the time though, he ended up talking to his new friend Richard, whom he had made friends with at some point during the night.

As per pub rules, it was a case of 'winner stays on.' The first game was between Fred/Olly and Reece/Ryan which was won by Reece's team quite easily. Jake and Jane were the ones up next to challenge them. Jane was surprisingly good, whilst Jake just aimed for anything he could hit. Reece and Ryan were on top throughout the whole game, until Ryan accidentally potted the white ball at the same time as the black. Jake and Jane celebrated whilst Ryan, who was super competitive, clearly shown that he was not happy.

A few more games passed and then the group went and sat back at a table. By this time, it was half past nine in the evening. They didn't plan on going home until closing though, which was about eleven o'clock.

Jake was talking to some of the other lads and Reece had popped to the toilet. Ryan and Jane were sitting opposite each other, and Jane kept looking at the scar on Ryan's forehead. The scar was about two or three centimetres in length and was slightly round in shape.

"How did you get your scar?" Jane asked out of curiosity.

"This one?" Ryan replied, pointing to his forehead. Jane nodded. Ryan looked up and down the table, to see if anyone was listening.

"Let's just say that me and Jake had a disagreement towards the end of our time at school." Ryan replied to Jane, rubbing his index finger over the scar. He was self-conscious of it, so he wasn't overly fond when people mentioned it.

"Jake did that to you?" Jane asked in shock. Ryan nodded. Jane turned to Jake and tapped him on the arm.

"You gave Ryan that scar?" Jane asked Jake. Jake was shocked, he had completely forgotten about the chances of that coming up at the get-together. Jake put his head down and remained quiet, clearly embarrassed.

"Yeah, he did," Fred added, chirping into the conversation. "Jake and Reece were having a fight and Jake was down on the floor. Jake looked to be down and out-"

"That's enough, I don't think we need to say anymore." Jake interrupted Fred, hoping to cover up any possibilities of his past coming up. He hadn't told Jane about any of this. He didn't mind her knowing but he wanted to keep any parts about him going to prison away from her. Fred sat quietly for a moment.

"No, carry on." Jane said, glaring at Jake wondering why he was so panicked by the story being told. There was a brief moment of silence as Fred clearly didn't feel comfortable continuing the conversation.

"Then, Jake gets up like a man rising from the dead," Olly continued the story, "And he picked up this big metal bar."

"Okay. That's enough now guys." Jake added, clearly getting agitated by the conversation. Jane hit Jake lightly on the arm and nodded at Olly to continue.

"Next thing we know, Jake swings for Reece and misses, then clouts Ryan around the head knocking him clean out." Olly concluded with a little chuckle. It was more of an awkward laugh when he saw the frustrated look on Jake's face.

Jane took a moment and then burst out into laughter just as Reece come back from the toilet.

"What have I missed?" Reece asked, curious as to

the reason behind Jane's hysterical laughter.

"Just telling the story of my scar." Ryan replied. Reece looked over at Jake and could see Jake's embarrassment.

"I never thought you had it in you," Jane said to Jake, punching him softly in the arm, "This man preaches peace like no other."

Jane continued to laugh. Jake smirked a bit to cover up his stressing, however, he did scratch his nose at the same time. It was clear he was starting to get anxious. The others laughed and joked about it for a bit, including Ryan. Then, Fred came out with a line which would completely change the whole atmosphere at the table.

"I forgot to ask by the way," Fred said to Jake in between his laughter, "How was it on the inside?"

Jake's eyes widened, glaring at Fred, and then looking back at Reece. Jane's laughter stopped abruptly.

"What do you mean, on the inside?" Jane asked, looking over at Jake. She subconsciously knew what they meant but couldn't bring herself to believe that her loving husband had kept something so big from her.

"Prison, had he not said?" Fred responded. Jake's head dropped and he slumped down in his chair. He was about to interrupt again but it was too late. Reece's face dropped as well. The damage had already been done.

"You went to prison Jake?" Jane asked sternly. She

was not impressed.

"Can we talk about this another time?" Jake asked Jane, not wanting to have an argument in front of the guys.

"No," Jane stated firmly, "How have you kept this from me for all these years?"

"We'll talk about it later." Jake replied, not impressed that the topic of his prison time had been brought into the conversation.

"No, you'll answer me now Jake." Jane replied again. She wasn't going to give up until she'd got an answer.

"I SAID WE'LL FUCKING TALK ABOUT IT AFTERWARDS. OKAY?" Jake shouted as he slammed the table with his right hand in a blend of both anger and irritation. The whole table went silent. Jane was stunned into silence by Jake's outburst. As was everyone else. Not as shocked as Jake though, who sat in silence for a brief moment. Then, Jake got up without saying a word and began to walk away.

"Sorry Jake," Fred shouted, "I didn't know."

"Fuck off Fred." Jake replied in temper. A comment he would later regret. They heard the pub door slam behind Jake as he stormed out of the pub.

Jake couldn't believe it. He jumped straight in a taxi and headed straight home. He was not looking forward to the conversation that he and Jane would be having, especially after his reaction. He wanted to text her but knew that he would need some time to calm down first.

FOLLOW IN MY FOOTSTEPS

Jake got into the house and locked the door behind him. He went and poured himself a glass of milk in the kitchen. He finished the glass and stood there, leaning up against the worktop, and stared at the glass. Then, a wave of pure anger came over Jake. Jake launched the glass at the floor causing it to shatter into various pieces. He stood there for a moment and then it dawned on him what he had just done.

Jake rushed to pick the glass up in a sheer panic and felt a sharp pain sweep across his hand. He had cut himself on the glass. Jake went straight to the sink and put his hand under the tap as blood started streaming out of the five-centimetre cut which ran across the palm of his right hand. Jake reached for the anti-septic wipes and the bandage which was in the cupboard to his right-hand side.

Jake left his hand in the water for a bit until the bleeding had calmed down. He then cleaned the wound and wrapped a bandage around his hand which left a bloody, red, mark on the bandage on the palm of his hand. Jake then went to get a dustpan and brush to clean up the glass, making sure to be extra careful. He took the dustpan outside and emptied it into the recycling bin.

Jake then walked back into the kitchen and looked down at the floor. There was a massive chip mark on the floor and a crack on the laminate tile. It was ruined.

Jake put his hand over his face and tears started

streaming out. Jake poured himself some water into a plastic cup to avoid any further damage in the case of another outburst. Jake never usually found himself getting this emotional but something in him seemed to have just snapped. Jake put his phone on charge next to his bed and lay down but couldn't sleep.

Jake picked up his phone and turned down the brightness to prevent his phone from blinding him. He opened his phone and went to text messages and started typing a message to Reece. 'Please make sure Jane gets home safe for me. Sorry for causing a scene.' Jake put his phone down only for it to buzz two minutes later to say he had a notification from Reece. 'No worries. She's on the way to her friends.' Jake sent a text saying 'Thank you' and then turned his phone off to go to sleep.

However, Reece had lied. All the other lads left not long after, but Jane stayed and started drinking more and more, matching Reece's levels of drinking. Reece was having a good time with Jane, so he told Jake that Jane was going to her friends to give him some peace of mind. He knew Jake would be stressed if he didn't know that Jane was safe.

They drank and they drank. The time was coming up to closing.

"How can you drink so much?" Jane asked, shocked by the way that Reece was just downing pint after pint.

"Plenty of practice." Reece responded. He laughed a little at first but then put his head down in shame and slowly moved the glass around in small circles, causing the contents to slowly wave against the side of the glass.

"What do you mean?" Jane asked. She could see that Reece was clearly disappointed in himself. But what for?

"I'm an alcoholic," Reece replied, taking another sip of his beer, "It's the only way I've been able to deal with all the shit I've been through."

Jane put her hand out and rested it on top of his to show him support. Reece looked back up at her and she quickly moved her hand away. Doing that had given her a funny feeling that she knew she was only meant to have for Jake. She blushed and Reece looked her straight in the eyes, trying to figure out what it meant.

At this point, both of them had drank enough to be able to know they were drunk. This wasn't just a drunk feeling though. Reece leaned over to Jane and kissed her lips. Jane didn't exactly stop him, but she pulled away, adjusting her hair afterwards.

"I'm so sorry Jane," Reece said, instantly apologetic and filled with regret, "I don't know what came over me."

"It's fine, don't worry about it." Jane said back, reassuring Reece. She didn't know what to make of it. It felt so wrong to her because of her being married to Jake. At the same time though, it felt right. Like it was meant to be. Just then, the bartender came over and told them that it was closing time. So, Reece and

Jane both made their way to the exit.

They got outside and the rain was coming down heavily. Reece got his jacket and covered both of their heads as they ran towards a taxi, which they got in together. Reece gave his address as the destination and then looked over at Jane.

"Where do you want dropping off?" He asked her. Jane paused for a moment.

"Can I stop at yours for tonight?" She asked nervously, "I don't think I can face Jake after his outburst earlier. I'll let him cool off."

Reece nodded and the driver took them both to Reece's house, following the sat-nav. The journey was around ten minutes.

When they got in, Reece poured himself and Jane a glass of water each. Reece then took Jane upstairs and shown her to his room. He planned on offering her the double bed in the main bedroom and he would take the single bed in the spare room.

When they got into the main bedroom though, no words were exchanged. Reece put the glasses of water on the side and shared a look with Jane. That was all it took.

They went straight at each other in a moment of drunken weakness and passion. Not once did Jake spring to mind. They both felt a connection there and it was only a matter of time until they acted on it, especially since they were under the same roof. Both of them betrayed Jake that night, but they didn't care. They would only realise the gravity of their actions in

FOLLOW IN MY FOOTSTEPS

the morning after they woke up.

7 MAINTAINING THE LIE

Sunday 25th June 2017, the morning after.
Jake's day

Jake woke up the next morning feeling lonely. He was expecting that Jane would have come back during the night, but she never did. Jake lay in bed scrolling through his phone for half an hour and contemplating calling or texting Jane. Jake would type out messages only to delete them straight after. In the end, Jake decided to give her some space.

After half an hour had passed, Jake checked the time. Quarter past nine. He knew he needed to get up. Jake climbed out of bed and hauled himself over to the bathroom to get himself washed. He spent ten minutes in the shower, cleaned his teeth, and went downstairs to make breakfast. After eating breakfast, Jake just found himself sitting around for an hour on end waiting for Jane to come home. She never did.

At eleven o'clock midday, Jake decided to go out and head into work on his own. He got fed up of waiting for Jane and needed to take his mind off things. When he got to work, he had the whole office to himself. It was a Sunday after all. The lads did have a pub league match, however, Jake didn't feel it was appropriate to go after his outburst the night before.

Jake got to work going through new stories which were coming in and putting his name down for the ones which he decided that he wanted to work through. Jane kept popping into his head though, and his concentration levels were up and down like a bouncy ball. He needed to put things right with Jane, but he had no idea how he could do that. Every time he thought about Jane, he would just block the thoughts out and would carry on working.

Jake wrote up two articles that day to be published throughout the week. He then filled out his overtime application and left it in the admin tray. Jake collected his belongings and took a glance at the clock before he left. Twenty-five minutes past three in the afternoon. He then made his way down the stairs and headed to his car. Jake drove the long route home. There were plenty of scenic roads which he could travel down and a few roads where he could really put his foot down to vent his frustrations.

Jake got home at ten past four. Jane still wasn't home. Jake tried not to think anything of it. She was probably still cooling off at her friends. At least, that's what he thought. 'She just needs time, she'll come around.'

Jake went to the fridge and got himself a bottle of beer. He took the cap off and sat down on the sofa. He turned the television on to see what was on. Jake put on a game show that he rather enjoyed and sat back, shouting out the answers as they flashed up on the screen. He was sure that he could be a competitor on the show and kept saying he would do it one day. He knew that he never would though. He didn't have the confidence to go on television in front of thousands of people.

Jake ordered himself a takeaway, as he couldn't be bothered to cook. Normally, Jane would do a Sunday roast for him. Jake didn't even know where to start cooking it, so ordering a Chinese was just easier for him. Jake tried to stay awake for as long as possible, as he wanted to see if Jane would come back. However, he ended up falling asleep.

Jane's day

Jane woke up next to Reece the morning after they had slept together. She rolled over to see his face and instantly felt an immeasurable amount of guilt. She couldn't believe what she had done.

She shot up straight out of the bed, realising that she hadn't got any clothes on, and grabbed Reece's top from off the floor and put it on. Reece was woken by the quilt being thrown over his head. He looked over and saw Jane standing there covered by his top.

"Morning." Reece said with a smile on his face. He didn't know how Jane felt, but after last night, he thought he had a good idea. There was clearly a connection. Jane just glared at him. Then the guilt flooded his emotions. He was still a bit drunk, but he soon realised what he had done.

"Oh fuck," Reece exclaimed, covering his face.

Jane put her hand over her face, in utter disbelief at the betrayal she had committed.

"Where's your bathroom?" Jane asked Reece.

"Just down the hall, on the right." Reece responded. The silence was unbearable, as was the thought of what they had done. Jane turned around and walked straight to the bathroom. Reece got up and got some clothes out which he put on. He tidied up the bed and folded Jane's clothes into a neat pile which he left outside the bathroom for her. Reece put his own clothes into the washing basket which was starting to get full. He hadn't got to do the washing for another two days yet. Reece then went downstairs and put the kettle on.

Jane heard Reece go downstairs and wiped away the tears that were forming in her eyes. She couldn't believe what she had done. At the same time, she was feeling just as guilty at the fact that she wasn't regretting it. She didn't know why she didn't regret it. Jane had to think of something though, she obviously couldn't tell Jake the truth. It would break him. Given his reaction last night, she had no clue how he would react to her being honest about her and Reece.

Jane opened the bathroom door to get her clothes from the bedroom to find them on the floor. She put them straight on and went downstairs to the kitchen to see Reece making two cups of tea.

"Any sugars?" Reece asked her sheepishly.

"Two please." Jane responded. Both of them were sheepish and blunt with each other, not really knowing what to say. They were both feeling the same. They felt guilty for what they had done and how they had betrayed Jake, but at the same time, they didn't have any regrets.

Reece handed Jane the tea which she accepted off him, grasping it with two hands, and blew into it to cool it down. Reece just drank out of it straight away. Jane looked at the time on the kitchen clock. Quarter to eleven.

"I bet Jake's wondering where I am." Jane said in a panic, putting her tea on the side.

"I told him you were going to a friend's house," Reece replied to Jane, calming her down, "He text me last night wanting me to make sure you got back safe."

"Oh, okay." Jane replied, feeling herself calm down slightly. She picked her tea back up. The atmosphere between them was uncomfortable.

"What happened last night was-" Reece started to say to Jane before being interrupted by her.

"A mistake," Jane told Reece abruptly, fearing what he was about to say next, "It should never have happened."

Reece was caught completely off guard. That was not the response he was expecting. It hurt him to feel rebuffed, but he understood why.

"We can't tell Jake," Jane told Reece as he looked down at the floor in disappointment, "Under no circumstances must he know."

Jane wanted to be sure that Reece wouldn't say anything. She knew she'd be lying to Jake, but she convinced herself it was for his own good. She knew that it would be easy to tell him the lie, however, the difficult part would come when she had to start maintaining the lie.

"He deserves to know," Reece responded, causing Jane to scowl over at him. "He has a right to know."

Jane panicked. She was furious at the same time. 'How could Reece possibly know what was right for Jake?' She needed to find a way to stop Reece from blabbering to Jake.

"You will not tell him." Jane told Reece firmly, in an authoritative manner.

"He deserves to know Jane." Reece replied to Jane, being just as firm in his response.

"You won't tell him," Jane replied, continuing to scowl at Reece, "If you do, you can trust me when I say that you'll regret it."

Reece froze. 'Did Jane really just threaten him?' He didn't know how to react. He didn't think Jane could be capable of carrying out any threats but the look on her face told him otherwise. Reece couldn't muster up any words in response to what she had said.

"Besides, it's your fault anyway," Jane added, realising she had Reece on the back foot, "You text him to say I was at my friend's. You could easily have stopped yourself, but you wanted this. You took advantage of me whilst I was drunk."

"That's a fucking lie!" Reece shouted, slamming his fist onto the worktop. Jane showed no fear of him, which frightened Reece even more.

"Who's Jake more likely to believe though?" Jane told Reece as she approached him. Reece felt like he was face to face with the devil in human form, "His caring wife? Or the bully who already has a literal reputation for kicking him whilst he's down."

Jane had a smugness to her face now. Reece couldn't think of a response. Jane looked over at the knife on the worktop and then back at Reece, instilling even more fear into him.

"So, what's it going to be?" Jane said to Reece, reaching into his trouser pocket and grabbing his phone which she then proceeded to wave in front of him, "You can call him now if you want?"

Jane wanted Reece to be as scared as he possibly could. If he thought she had the potential to act on her threats, he wouldn't even contemplate disobeying her. She had a feeling of control too, one that she liked. All she needed to know now was whether or not Reece believed her or whether he thought she was bluffing.

Reece took the phone out of Jane's hand, slightly

FOLLOW IN MY FOOTSTEPS

trembling. He unlocked his phone and looked up at Jane who was staring him dead in the eyes. Reece thought about it for a second. 'Should he tell Jake? If he did, what would Jane do? She's clearly ready to do anything to keep her marriage alive.'

Reece took a gulp and locked his phone. Jane felt a wave of relief come over her, but she didn't show it. She was overwhelmed by this feeling of control. This feeling of power. Meanwhile, Reece felt fear. He was scared of what Jane was capable of. Both of them finished their drinks and then Reece grabbed his car keys.

"Do you want me to drop you off?" Reece asked Jane, trembling slightly with nerves.

"Drop me at JoJo's salon in town," Jane told Reece, needing to keep up this show of power, "But first I'm going to clean my teeth."

Jane went up the stairs and into the bathroom. Whilst up there, she could take a moment to snap out of this new persona that she had embodied to scare Reece. Deep down, she was full of guilt. Jane started telling herself that it was Reece's fault and not her own, but nothing could fully suppress the guilt she had.

Once she'd finished cleaning her teeth and brushed her hair, she headed down the stairs. She embodied this new, power-hungry, persona that she had invented. She put her shoes on, and Reece opened the door. Jane walked through and got into Reece's car.

Neither of them said anything to each other on the drive into town. Reece was too sheepish and scared to say anything, and Jane was battling the inner guilt she had. She continued trying to maintain this strong personality to stop Reece from even considering spilling the truth to Jake.

Reece pulled up outside the salon. Jane didn't say a word to Reece. She got out of the car, grabbed her bag with her purse, and headed straight for the salon. Reece took off as quickly as he could. As soon as Jane heard Reece's car move away, she was able to breathe a sigh of relief.

Jane walked straight past the salon and headed into a nearby café where she sat and had a few coffees. She needed to get herself focused and distract herself from the fact that she had cheated on Jake with his newfound best friend. Jane also started feeling guilty for threatening Reece. Jane spent the rest of the day trying to convince herself that she was in the right for doing what she had done.

Jane left the café at half past four and wanted to go home. She wanted to see Jake and check if he was okay. At the same time, she couldn't bring herself to face him. Not only had he lied to her and shouted and sworn at her in a pub full of people, but she had cheated on him as well.

In the end, Jane decided to go and visit her friend for a bit. They sat and had a few glasses of wine together and relaxed. Jane wanted to explain her situation but didn't want her friend to think any less of her. Also, all of her friends were gossipers and something like this would spread around like wildfire.

Jane left her friends at eleven and started to make her way back home. It was a thirty-minute walk so it was a good job that there wasn't any rain. The closer and closer she got to being home, the more worried she got. She didn't want to go back and face Jake. At the same time, she knew that she had too eventually.

At half past eleven in the evening, Jake was woken by the sound of the front door being unlocked with a key. He got to his feet and went out to open the front door. As he came out of the living room, Jane was shutting the front door. She knew Jake was there but didn't say anything to him.

"Hey," Jake sheepishly said to Jane hoping to get some sort of response, "Do you want to talk?"

Jane didn't even bother giving Jake a reaction. She slipped her shoes off and went straight up the stairs. She couldn't face him after what she had done. It was nothing to do with what he did by this point, she was embarrassed and ashamed. So, she took herself straight to bed, knowing Jake wouldn't follow her up.

Jake went back into the living room and lay on the sofa. He fluffed up one of the pillows and wrapped himself up in the blanket. He expected that he would be sleeping there for a while from this point on.

Jake lay on the sofa for a while, unable to sleep. It wasn't a case of that he wasn't comfortable, it was the fact that Jane didn't even say anything to him when she got in. There was no reaction. No anger. Nothing.

Just void of emotion.

Thoughts and questions circled through Jake's head. 'Does she still love me?' was the prominent question that kept coming around. He would only be able to get an answer to that though if he asked her directly. He wasn't ready to do that just yet. Jake gave it another half an hour and then checked the time on his phone. Half past one. Jake still couldn't sleep. Jake grabbed the remote for his games console and played for an hour until he physically couldn't keep his eyes open. He thought about asking Reece for some advice, but he knew Reece would probably be asleep by now.

Jake woke up the next morning at eight o'clock. He was starting work at nine o'clock, so he wanted to give himself plenty of time to get some breakfast and get ready for work. He went up the stairs to get some clothes out of his room and was quiet, so he did not disturb Jane. Little to his knowledge, Jane hadn't slept all night. She was still awake and just pretended to be asleep.

Jake picked his clothes up and his work bag from out of the room and took his things into the bathroom where he got changed and ready. He then went downstairs and poured himself a glass of milk. He usually drank tea, but he didn't want to boil the kettle in case he woke Jane up. He ate what he could of his breakfast and then headed back upstairs.

He went into the bedroom and kissed Jane on the head before leaving. Jane was hit with so much guilt that it was unbearable. She left it for a moment and then went to get up to say goodbye to Jake. As she got up, she heard the door close. Jane went to the window where she saw Jake's car reverse off the drive and drive up the street.

Jake got to work and waited for Reece to arrive. He desperately needed Reece's advice and a shoulder to cry on. Jake waited and waited but Reece didn't show.

"Where's Reece today?" Jake asked the boss, curious as to where his friend was.

"He's called in sick," The boss replied, "Said it was to do with something dodgy yesterday."

Jake instantly texted Reece to check on him and to wish him a speedy recovery. All he got back was a thumbs-up emoji. Jake tried not to think anything of it and put it down to Reece's food poisoning. Jake finished his day of work and stopped off at Reece's house on the way home but got no answer from knocking at the door. Jake waited for a minute or two and then left and headed back home.

Reece was in the house though, feeling perfectly well. He couldn't stand to face Jake because of what he'd done. Jake was meant to be one of his closest friends and he'd let him down. Reece also worried about seeing Jake in case he said anything about what had happened between him and Jane. He knew he would struggle not to say anything about what happened. Therefore, Reece considered that it was best if he didn't see Jake at all. How he was going to manage that with work was another story. He could only pull a sick day for one more day before it became suspicious. Reece had already started applying for local jobs on his phone so that he could try and get out of the situation as fast as possible.

Jake got home and saw that Jane's car wasn't on the drive, so she wasn't in. He didn't know when she would be back but knew she would come back when she was ready to talk. Jake went upstairs and saw that one of his overnight bags was missing. He opened the drawers to see some of Jane's clothes were gone too. Jake slammed the drawers in frustration and stormed out of the bedroom. Jane was gone. Jake would have to fend for himself for a while.

Jake cooked himself some dinner. Cooked some dinner is an exaggeration given that all he did was toast some bread and heat up some beans. He didn't eat it all anyways. He was too angry and upset. Jake took himself to bed early and tried to get to sleep. He decided to sleep in the bed upstairs, given that it was obvious that Jane wouldn't be coming back for a while. He checked his phone to see if he had any messages or calls from Jane or Reece, but there was nothing. By now, he was used to seeing that he had no notifications. Jake eventually dropped off to sleep out of pure tiredness from the lack of sleep from the night before.

Jake woke up again the next morning to an empty space next to him. Jake felt even worse, but expected that Reece would be at work and back to his usual self. So, he hauled himself out of bed, got dressed and cleaned, had his breakfast and his usual morning cup of tea, and went to work.

Jake waited again for Reece but no sign of him at all. He'd had the day off sick once again. Jake started to worry that he'd upset Reece with his outburst as well. He texted Reece saying 'Can we talk?' but never got a response.

Jake finished work and contemplated stopping off at Reece's on the way home but ultimately decided against it. Everyone seemed to be avoiding him after his outburst. Jake realised that he needed to get a hold of his outbursts as they were getting worse. The outburst at the table, smashing glasses and slamming drawers. This was nothing like him.

When Jake got home, he looked up anger management courses online and booked in to see a therapist, so that he had someone who he could talk to. He was never usually a talker. Hopefully, this would help him. At this point, Jake just wanted Jane back.

8 PUSHING AWAY

Jake called his boss and said he needed some time off due to some home-life issues around his marriage. His boss, who was naturally a very understanding person, told Jake to take all the time he needed. Jake didn't want to have too long off. He agreed to take the week off and go back to work on Monday 3rd July. In the meantime, Reece returned to work for a few days only to find that Jake wasn't there. By the time Friday came around, Reece managed to get a role at a newspaper company on the other side of town. He started there on the Monday that Jake returned to work.

Jake went in and just assumed that Reece was still off sick. It must have been serious for him not to contact Jake at all. Then, the boss called Jake into his office to break the news to him that Reece had left.

"What?" Jake asked, confused as to what he had just heard, "Did he give any reason as to why?"

"He just told me that he couldn't cope, and another outlet offered him some reduced hours," The boss replied, clearly disappointed in Reece's departure, "I take it that he never told you that he planned on leaving."

"No, I haven't spoken to him all week," Jake replied, "I don't know what's happening with him, but I'll find out."

Jake left the office, and a sense of complete loneliness washed over him. He had lost his wife and his best friend all because of one night. So, like he did when Eric died, he threw himself into his work.

Over the next couple of days, he wrote some of the best articles of his career. He stayed on late at work and made sure that the work he put out was his best. On Wednesday, Jake returned home from a long day of work. He pulled onto the drive and saw that the blinds were shut, which he found odd as he rarely shut them.

Jake walked into the house and took off his shoes, which he kicked towards the wall. He looked over at the living room to see a glimpse of light shining through. Curious, Jake went to investigate.

He slowly opened the living room door and walked in. Jane was sat on the sofa. Jake joined her, but sat on the other side of the sofa. Jane didn't acknowledge that Jake had walked in at first. Jake sat for a few moments to see if Jane would say anything.

He couldn't think of any words to say. Clearly his 'Hey, do you want to talk?' that he used last time was of no use, so he needed to think of something new. Jake remained seated on the sofa for another thirty seconds and then looked over at Jane again. She had tears welling up in her eyes.

"Look, I know there's nothing I can say," Jake told Jane with a choke to his voice as he fought back tears, "I'm sorry I never told you."

Jane sat in silence, fighting back tears herself. Jake had no idea. He came in to apologise to her, and she couldn't even give him a response.

"I get that you don't want to talk to me, I screwed up and I'm sorry. I guess I've spent so long pushing away all those horrible memories that I didn't want anyone to know," Jake added, "I didn't want you to think any less of me. I'm sorry."

Realising that there was nothing else he could say, Jake got up from the sofa. He took one last look at Jane, who was slowly losing the battle against the tears in her eyes, and walked towards the door. As he opened the door, Jane spoke.

"Just explain it all to me," Jane said, having to take gasps for air through the emotion, "Tell me everything."

"Of course, no more secrets," Jake told Jane as he smiled slightly at her, "I'll put the kettle on."

Jake walked out of the room and shut the door behind him. Jane, gasping for air, instantly reached for a tissue to wipe her eyes and blow her nose. Her emotions felt so raw, but she couldn't get too emotional in case Jake started suspecting something. Jake was the kind of person who would ask questions about everything and would not be happy until he got an answer. That's why it was going to be so hard for her to keep this dark secret. Jake had literally just told her no more secrets, yet this was one she needed to keep for the sake of their marriage. Even though Jake couldn't give her children, Jane loved Jake. She had no idea what she would do without him. He helped her out of a dark place, and she helped him.

Jake entered the room holding two cups of tea. He passed one to Jane and kept one for himself.

Jake proceeded to explain everything to Jane about the incident that led to him going to prison. He told her about how badly Reece used to bully him and what they used to do to him. Jane was in shock. Then he told her about how he hit Ryan with the bar and how he didn't share the full truth with the Police because he wanted to take the blame. Jane felt absolutely heartbroken for Jake.

Jake started to well up with tears and emotion when he told her about Eric, the man he met in prison. Jane was stunned. She knew about the article, but she was never aware of the connection that Jake and Eric shared. Jake broke down into a flood of tears when he told her how he died.

"He obviously gave you his story as a final gesture," Jane said, crying but also trying to comfort Jake, "He'll be so proud of everything you've achieved. How far you've come."

"I know," Jake replied, wiping tears from his eyes using the sleeve of his coat, "He never got a good chance at life though. He never got a second chance."

"That's not your fault. Eric felt the way that he felt. There was nothing you could have done about that," Jane told Jake trying to soothe him, "Deep down, he will always be with you."

Jake nodded in agreeance, but he did still blame himself for Eric's death all these years later.

"If I hadn't of wrote that article, maybe he'd still be alive." Jake told Jane, putting his head into his hands.

"That article was his gift to you. He knew it'd take you to success, that's why he gave it you," Jane put her arm around Jake as he continued to sob further, "And you redeemed him with that article. That was what he wanted."

Jake wiped away his tears again. Jane passed him a tissue which he used to blow his nose. Whilst he knew she was right, he couldn't help but blame himself. He wanted to use the article to work his way up the chain quicker, he never thought it would end up the way it did. 'Maybe Eric planned to kill himself all along and it was just the timing.'

"How are you able to forgive me so easily?" Jake asked Jane, putting his head on her shoulder and taking hold of her hand, which was on her leg, "I lied to you, and I spoke to you like shit."

"We all have our weaknesses. Clearly, that one is

yours. While I didn't appreciate how you spoke to me, I know now that your emotions must've been racing," Jane said to Jake, fighting off the guilt she was feeling, "But why didn't you feel like you could tell me?"

"I thought you'd see me as a criminal, and that you'd want nothing to do with me," Jake replied, "When I got out, I swore to myself that I wouldn't tell another soul."

Jane finally started to understand Jake. She could understand why he acted the way he did sometimes.

"We've still got that weekend away this weekend if you still want to go?" Jane told Jake, thinking that this would ease his pain. Jake looked up at her and smiled. She always knew what to say to cheer him up.

"I'd like that a lot." Jake told Jane, smiling through teary eyes. Finally, they were starting to get back on track. They'd hit a few bumps in the road, but they always found a way through. Jake felt like he could relax a lot more now that there were no more secrets between them. At least, none as far as he knew.

The two sat and had some dinner together and then went upstairs to pack. After all, they were leaving for their weekend trip on Friday. Whilst they were packing, Jane asked Jake about what she had missed in their time apart.

"Nothing much really," Jake replied, "Although me and Reece aren't talking."

"Why not?" Of course, she had a good idea as to why they had stopped talking. However, Jane could sense the sadness in Jake's voice as he said it.

"I have no idea. After my outburst at the get-together, he just stopped talking to me," Jake replied whilst he folded up his clothes to put into a pile, "Then he quit at the newspaper."

Jane stopped folding as she was struck by surprise. Maybe he had taken her threats seriously. She felt a massive wave of relief knowing that she wasn't going to have to worry about him telling Jake about their one-night stand.

"Maybe it's for the best then," Jane said to Jake which left him slightly confused, "Obviously he didn't care enough about your friendship to tell you."

"True. It's still gutting though, I honestly thought he'd changed." Jake replied as he continued to fold top after top.

"Some people don't change. Those people aren't worth chasing." Jane told Jake in response. She obviously wanted to push Jake away from having any contact with Reece at all. Jake wasn't having it though. He may have nodded to her in agreeance, but now that he had started to patch things up with Jane, he wanted to patch things up with Reece as well.

They finished folding the clothes and then both got ready for bed. For the first time in what had felt like forever, Jake was actually going to share a bed with Jane.

After a while, the two cuddled up and dropped off to sleep. Well, Jake dropped straight off to sleep. Jane stayed awake being eaten up by the guilt of what she had done. The fact that she was having to keep it from Jake was eating her up. At the same time, putting on this act of everything being okay was just exhausting for her.

The next morning, Jake had the usual routine as normal. He gave Jane a kiss and left for work. Today he wasn't going to be working overtime. He wasn't doing that for Jane though, he had other plans for after work. Jake wanted to speak to Reece. Jake texted Reece once during the day to ask him why he hadn't been in touch but didn't hear anything back. Jake wanted to patch up his issues with Reece before he left with Jane for the weekend.

Jake finished off the article he had been working on for the day and left on time. He texted Jane to say he was going to be late back. She wasn't best pleased but the less time he spent with her, the less time she had to fight off her secret.

Jake got into his car and drove straight to Reece's house. He saw Reece's car on the drive and, given that the only place Reece walked too was the pub, Jake was able to narrow down Reece's location one of two places. His house, or the Fradley's arms.

Jake knocked on Reece's door. No signs of life. He looked through the letterbox, but there was nothing. Then, Reece's neighbour was walking down their drive and was looking at Jake rather suspiciously.

"Can I help you?" The neighbour asked, holding the newspaper.

"Yes, sorry. I'm just looking for my friend who lives here. Have you seen him?" Jake replied. The neighbour looked at Reece's house and then back at Jake.

"Same place as usual, he's at the pub. I saw him walk there about forty minutes ago." The neighbour responded, clearly unimpressed by Reece's day-drinking antics.

"Thank you, what's your name?" Jake asked, trying to be friendly.

"It's Leonard, Len for short." The neighbour responded. Jake smiled.

"I'm Jake," He said back, "Pleasure to meet you."

The two smiled at each other for a moment, then Len went into his house. Jake got into his car and headed to the Fradley's arms.

Jake pulled up and could see the lads through the glass window. He felt a bit disappointed. 'Why hadn't they invited him to the pub?' Jake had felt like he was a part of the group. Jake turned off his engine and walked into the pub. He got a pint from the bar and went to the table.

"Hey guys," Jake opened up with, "Before anything else is said, I want to apologise about how I reacted the last time we were out. I was out of line."

Reece froze. He didn't know how to react. It was a bit tense for a moment, and then Olly broke the ice.

"It's lucky there were no metal bars around," Olly joked, "I thought you was going to deck poor Fred."

"Yeah, I shat myself a little bit." Fred joked. Jake laughed, Reece was still trying to figure out how Jake had found out that they were at the pub. He hadn't invited him, and he thought he'd made it clear that he didn't want to see him again. Reece was overwhelmed with a mix of guilt and fear, and it didn't go unnoticed.

"You okay Reece?" Jason asked, "You look like you've seen a ghost."

Reece stayed frozen.

"He's probably just shocked to see me, right?" Jake said, punching Reece in the arm lightly, "It's been a while hasn't it mate? How've you been?"

"Good, yeah," Reece said to Jake, seemingly stuck in some form of trance, "You?"

"Yeah, I've been good thanks," Jake replied, snapping his fingers in front of Reece's eyes, "You sure everything's okay?"

Reece snapped out of his trance and apologised. They all got back to talking, laughing, and joking. Reece however felt out of it. His sole focus now was to not slip the news out to Jake about what had happened between him and Jane. Especially after what Jane had done.

"Where's Ryan at?" Jake asked, noticing his unusual absence from the group.

"Not sure, nobodies been able to raise him for the last few days," Olly answered, "We haven't seen him since last Thursday It's almost as if he's dead to the world."

"Maybe he's just having some time away, I'm sure he'll be back around." Jason added. Reece sniffled as if he was about to start crying.

"What's up mate?" Jake asked Reece, putting his hand on his shoulder.

"Nothing I'm fine, can I talk to you for a second outside?" Reece asked Jake, picking up his pint.

"Sure," Jake replied, walking with Reece away from the table. He turned to look at Jason who just shrugged.

"What's going on?" Jake asked.

"Look, I've left the newspaper outlet mate. I've stopped talking to you because I want to focus on myself for a bit. Could you just give me a bit of space?" Reece told Jake abruptly. Jake was stunned.

"I'm sorry. What?" Jake asked, completely baffled by Reece.

"You heard me Jake," Reece replied, putting his head down, "I need some space."

This was completely out of character for Reece. Something was majorly off. Reece walked back into the pub where he re-joined the lads and left Jake standing outside. Jake watched on through the window as he saw Reece re-join the table and continue laughing and joking with the others.

Jake started to feel himself getting angry again. In a loss of temper, he launched his glass at the wall, painting it with beer. A couple of people smoking at the door watched on. Jake looked over at them as they whispered about him.

"You got something to say?" Jake shouted at them. They didn't respond, they just turned the other way.

Jake stormed off to his car and got in, starting the engine. He put his foot to the floor, using his accelerator to vent his frustration, and drove back to his house. It was a shock that he never got pulled over.

Jake stormed into the house and Jane was waiting up for him.

"Where have you been?" Jane asked Jake. He had no idea of the time.

"I went looking for Reece," Jake said as he walked into the kitchen, pacing backwards and forwards and fidgeting with anything he could get his hands on, "He said he wants space and doesn't want to see me anymore."

Jane was shocked but relieved at the same time. Her tactics had paid off, clearly, Reece wasn't going to tell Jake anything about them.

"I told you he wasn't worth chasing." Jane told Jake, giving him a hug to calm him down.

"I just don't know what I've done wrong. I apologised to all the lads for how I acted, and I didn't even swear at them," Jake started to rant, "Except for Fred but he made a laugh and a joke about it as per usual."

Jane gave Jake a hug, "It's not worth stressing over. Look at the time, let's get some food."

Jake looked at the clock, quarter past seven, he'd finished work at five o'clock.

"Sorry I'm so late," Jake apologised to Jane, "I went looking for answers. Wish I'd never found them."

Jane let go of Jake and went and got the Pizza menu. She knew it was one of his many favourites. They ordered from the local pizza place and stuck a film on the television. Once the film had finished, Jane got up to go to bed.

"Goodnight." She told Jake as she kissed him.

"I won't be far behind; I'm just going to check the news." Jake replied to Jane. She smiled at him, walking out of the room and shutting the door behind her.

Jake switched over to the local news, and after a few minutes, an announcement was made.

"In breaking news now, Police have just announced that earlier this morning they found a man's body by the old windmill in the forestry area," The news presenter announced, "No further details have been shared of the man yet other than they believe him to be in his mid-thirties. Police are treating it as suspicious with a cause of death yet to be determined."

"Always bad news." Jake said to himself quietly as he turned the television off. Jake headed up the stairs and went to the bathroom. He got himself ready and then went to bed. He tucked himself in and rolled over to put his arm around Jane. He gave her a kiss on the cheek and they both fell to sleep.

They were both excited for their weekend away. 'What could possibly go wrong?'

9 CAUGHT

Jake woke up first the next morning. His first feeling was one of excitement at their weekend away. Jake slipped out of bed, put some pyjamas on, and quietly headed downstairs. He wanted to surprise Jane with breakfast in bed. Whilst he could only do beans on toast primarily, his time on his own had taught him the skill of cooking bacon. Jake thought it was brilliant that he could cook more than one meal now.

Jane woke up whilst Jake was downstairs and was feeling sick. She'd been getting morning sickness the past few days but was trying to ignore it. She put it down to stress. 'Jake can't have kids' was what Jane kept thinking to herself, so she couldn't be pregnant.

Unless?

No, of course not. Jane put a dressing gown on and made her way downstairs to find Jake in the middle of cooking breakfast.

"Ah damn it," Jake said, gutted at the surprise being ruined, "Was I too loud? It was meant to be a surprise."

"Aww, how sweet," Jane replied with a smile as she kissed Jake on the cheek, "I'm sure it'll taste amazing either way."

Jake smiled back at Jane as she reached for a glass out of the cupboard. Jane filled the glass with some water and stood at the other end of the kitchen to Jake.

"Go back to bed if you want," Jake told Jane, "I'll bring it up to you."

Jane smiled at Jake once again and went back upstairs. She didn't want to say much because of her sickness. The last thing she wanted was to throw up and Jake find out. He had got enough on his plate without knowing that Jane wasn't feeling well. Jane did as she was told, going to their bedroom and tucking herself back into bed. Jake brought her breakfast in and a round of toast for himself – he wasn't very hungry. He'd also made two cups of tea which he brought up with him.

Jane ate most of the breakfast that Jake had made her and was pleasantly surprised. Jake's cooking had come on leaps and bounds whilst she had been gone.

"Wow," Jane complimented Jake's cooking, "Maybe I should leave you to fend for yourself more often."

"Please don't," Jake laughed, "It was horrible

having to learn to cook."

Jane laughed back at him. Jake took the plates down and washed them up. He came back up with another cup of tea. It was unlike Jake to do this, so he was clearly trying to get back onto Jane's good side. She felt bad that Jake clearly thought he was the one who had messed up, but she couldn't tell him the truth. She'd been keeping the truth from him for four days, two weeks if you count the time she was away, and she was getting better at it.

"Right, I think it's time we got up and ready to go." Jake told Jane as he came back up the stairs. Jane looked at the time. Twenty-five minutes past nine. Jake wanted to leave nice and early so they would have a longer time there. The two got showered and ready to go, making sure they had everything packed in their bags. Jake loaded the bags into the boot of his car. Once they had checked that everything had been packed away and all the electrics were switched off, they locked the door and left for the weekend.

It was going to be a three-hour drive to get to their destination. Granted there would be a few problems with other drivers on the road but Jane was used to Jake's passion for driving by now. They were on the motorway, about two hours into the drive when Jane complained about needing the toilet. Luckily, Jake had spotted a service station coming up in a few miles, so he exited the motorway there and pulled into the car park.

They went into the large glass building and Jane

rushed to find the toilets. Jake followed behind but he wasn't in as big of a rush. Jake finished in the toilet and waited for Jane outside. The two looked around the shops for a bit and then Jake decided to go and buy hot drinks for them for the drive that they had ahead of them.

"I'm going to get two cups of tea for the road," Jake told Jane, "Could you pick up some snacks?"

"Sure thing, what do you fancy?" Jane asked Jake, looking around for which shop had the best selection.

"I'll just have some crisps or something. Surprise me." Jake told Jane as he walked off to go and join the queue for the hot drinks. Jane went in and started looking around, taking time to look at a range of books and snacks. Whilst looking through the store, Jane came across some pregnancy tests. She looked over at Jake to see if he was looking. Fortunately, he was in the middle of ordering the drinks for them both. Jane picked up a box of pregnancy tests, just to rule anything out. She gathered a few snacks for the road and an intriguing-looking book too. She paid for them on her card and shoved the pregnancy tests into her handbag, resting the book and crisps on top of them. As she left the store, Jake was just walking away with a drink in each hand.

"All sorted?" Jake asked Jane with a smile on his face.

"Yep," Jane responded, still happy that they were getting some quality time together, "Got everything we need."

The two took a relaxed walk back to the car. They got in and Jane got the snacks out of her bag. Jake noticed she had bought a new book but didn't see the pregnancy tests underneath.

"Is that a new one?" He asked, motioning towards the book.

"Oh," Jane said, caught out by his question, "Yeah, it is. Not sure what it's about but it looked good."

Jake just nodded to acknowledge what she had said and started the car. A massive feeling of relief flushed through Jane. She was worried for a second that he would see the pregnancy tests and get suspicious. They re-joined the motorway and, whilst driving, the news was playing on the radio in the background.

"And now in other news," The radio host announced, "The body of a thirty-four-year-old man was found by the old windmill today after he had been stabbed to death a few days prior to the discovery. The man, who has not yet been named-"

"Always negative news nowadays," Jane said as she switched the source from the radio to her Bluetooth, "Why can't people just get on."

"I know," Jake replied, "I can't even begin to think what would have to be going through someone's head to do something like that."

"A really bad day I guess." Jane added, looking over at Jake.

"Maybe," Jake said back to Jane, "Still doesn't

excuse it."

The two carried on with their journey, with only thirty minutes left until they arrived. They got off the motorway and carried on following the sat-nav until they arrived. Jake had all the codes, so he checked them in. They then went and found their cabin. Number forty-four. Jake pulled onto the one-car drive and got out of his car. Jake stopped for a moment, taking in a breath of the fresh air. Jane got out of the car too, stretching her arms and legs out.

"Here we are," Jake said with his hands on his hips, "Home sweet home for the next few days."

Jane smiled and reached into the car to grab the envelope which had the keys to the cabin.

"Catch!" Jane shouted, throwing the keys over the roof of the car to Jake who managed to catch them. Jake turned around and unlocked the door to their new temporary residence. Jake stepped in and looked around the wooden cabin in awe. It was beautiful. Jane went and stood by the glass doors which led out onto the balcony. It had two bedrooms, an ensuite, a bathroom, a living and dining area, a kitchen, and the balcony which featured a hot tub. The whole cabin sported a rustic look which provided a cosy feel to them both.

After taking some time to look around the cabin, Jake went outside and got the bags which he then bought into the living space of the cabin. Jane then carried them into the bedroom where she started taking clothes out and organising them into separate piles. Jake's tops, her tops. Jake's trousers, her trousers. Jake's underwear, her underwear. They divvied the wardrobe and drawers in half where they put their clothes separately.

Once they'd got everything sorted, they went out to the on-site convenience store to get supplies for the next few days. Teabags, milk, bread, cereal, and so on. They returned to the cabin which was only a fifteen-minute walk. However, it was mostly uphill on the way back, so it was an exerting fifteen minutes. They got back in and chilled out on the sofas for a bit. They'd seen a nice little restaurant near the main activity centre, so they were going to go there for dinner. They agreed on going down at about seven o'clock in the evening. They started getting ready at half past five in the evening, taking a nice warm shower together before getting changed.

Jake wore a polo shirt, black jeans, and a pair of black trainers. He was going to wear his white ones but didn't want to ruin them on the walk there. It had rained between them going to the store and them getting ready, so they were likely to get dirty from the rain. Jane wore a slim red dress which Jake stood staring at when she first put it on. They walked down and asked for a table for two. Jake ordered the steak whilst Jane opted for chicken and chips. It wasn't the best food, standard 'pub grub.' They took a little venture around the arcade before heading back to the cabin at half past nine.

They got in and Jane was too tired to stay up, so

she took herself off to bed early. Jake stayed up watching an old comedy about two men looking for their car – one of his favourite comedies it turns out. Jane was getting ready and shut the door behind her. She went into the toilet, grabbing the pregnancy tests out of her handbag. Jane contemplated opening them for a minute. 'Did she really want to know the result?'

In the end, she decided on doing the test. She did what she needed to do and then left it on the sink in the ensuite toilet. She cleaned her teeth and took off her makeup.

She went back in to check the test and couldn't believe her eyes. Two lines. Clear as day. The test was positive. Jane was pregnant. Jane started to panic. She threw the test out of the window and pretended like it had never happened. She stuffed the tests into her underwear drawer and covered them up. She got into bed but couldn't sleep.

Jake come into bed at midnight and Jane was still awake, though she pretended to be asleep. Jake got into his pyjamas, climbed into bed, and put his arm around her. Jake was snoring within ten minutes. For Jane that was it, no sleep for now. She gave it an hour and then she went into the other bedroom in the hope that she would get some sleep in there. After another twenty minutes, she finally dropped off to sleep out of pure tiredness.

Jake woke up early the next morning to find Jane wasn't lying next to him. He took a brief look around the cabin and noticed her sleeping in the other room.

Realising it was probably because of his snoring, he quietly made his way into the kitchen and left her to sleep. Jake decided to take the rubbish out. There wasn't much of it, but it was only a small bin, so it was getting full after they'd emptied all the packaging from their shopping into there. Jake quietly exited the cabin, walking around to the outdoor bins. On the way there he spotted an oddly shaped, white-coloured, object on the floor near to one of the windows of their cabin.

Jake reached down and saw it was a pregnancy test. 'Surely not' Jake thought to himself. After all, he couldn't have kids. He wanted to be sure it wasn't Jane's but how could he even bring that into the conversation?

All of a sudden, he heard a shout. It was Jane. Jake quickly shoved the test into his pocket and turned around.

"Morning," She shouted out of the window, "Never thought I'd see the day where you took the rubbish out."

Jake laughed and put his middle finger up in a joking way. Jane laughed and shut the window and went off to start cooking breakfast. Jake put the rubbish bag into the outdoor bins and then returned to the cabin where Jane was stood in the kitchen boiling the kettle. Jake walked in and sat on the sofa, trying to digest whether it was true or not. 'Could Jane actually be pregnant?' Jake was so deep in thought that he never even heard Jane talking to him.

From out of nowhere, he was hit in the face with a tea towel.

"Earth to Jake," Jane said in an alien-like accent, "What do you want for breakfast?"

"Oh," Jake replied, trying to get back to reality, "I'm not that hungry."

"Same here," Jane replied, "That meal last night was huge."

"Yeah. It was." Jake was a man of few words at the moment. He was still deep in thought despite the wake-up call from the flying tea towel.

"Is everything okay?" Jane asked. She could tell something was up with Jake as she came and sat down next to him.

"Everything's fine," Jake replied, standing up, "Do you fancy going to the hot tub?"

"Of course," Jane smiled back at Jake, standing up with him, "I'll get my bikini on."

They both got into their swimwear and went out to the balcony where Jake figured out how to turn the hot tub on. Once it was up to temperature, Jake slowly lowered himself into the tub followed by Jane. The two relaxed for an hour. Jake got up to go and make some drinks for them both and go to the toilet. Whilst he was in the ensuite, Jake rummaged through drawers and cupboards looking for pregnancy tests with no luck. Jake looked through Jane's bag too, making sure to put everything back as he found it. Nothing. He knew he couldn't be too long, so he went to make the drinks and returned to Jane in the hot tub.

They relaxed there for another hour until Jane got out.

"We'll be turning to shrimp at this rate," Jane told Jake as she gave him a kiss, "You coming?"

Jake nodded and climbed out of the hot tub. Jane leaned up against the balcony for a moment, observing the view. Jake stood behind her and wrapped his arms around her. He forgot about his worries in that brief moment. All he could focus on was his wife. Jane turned around and grabbed his hands, kissing him again before moving it on to the bedroom.

They both lay on the bed for a while afterwards. Jane rolled over to face Jake and smiled at him. Jake smiled back.

"I'm going for a shower," Jane told Jake as she got up, "I'll see you in there?"

"Of course." Jake replied with his smile still covering his face. He watched Jane as she went into her underwear drawer until he saw the corner of what looked to be a white box. Jane shut the drawer and leaned over and kissed Jake. She then went into the bathroom, making sure to see that Jake noticed her not locking the door. Jake waited for the shower to turn on and the shower door to close, and then he reached over to her drawer and opened it.

He sifted through her underwear and spotted the box at the bottom of the drawer. Pregnancy tests. Jake went and got the test out of the pocket of his jeans which were on the floor in the corner of the room. The test matched the one pictured on the box. Jake knew it. Jane was pregnant.

'But how?'

He couldn't give her children unless it was by some miracle. He still didn't have enough to question her on it though. Jake needed more evidence. Jake put her underwear back over the box and shut the drawer. He then joined her in the shower.

By one o'clock in the afternoon, Jake and Jane were sat in the living room watching television. They were going to go out but opted to stay in for a while and go out for tea in the village. Jake saw Jane texting on her phone and saw her put it back down. A while later, Jane stood up.

"I'll be back in a minute." She told Jake, as she walked towards the bedroom, presumably going to use the toilet. Jake waited to hear the door shut and then picked up Jane's phone. Whilst he had always respected her privacy, she'd kept the pregnancy tests from him, so he wanted an answer. He went to unlock her phone, having seen her passcode ten minutes prior, but he paused for a moment. He weighed it up in his head and ended up putting the code in. Seven, One, Zero, Three. A random series of numbers but one that, for some reason, Jane easily remembered.

Jake hadn't got long so he went straight to messages. Top of the list was Reece. 'How odd?' Jake thought to himself. 'Why would she be messaging

Reece? How did she even get his number?' Jake kept digging. He clicked into the conversation to see a long string of messages. Then, a message from the twenty-seventh of June.

'We need to tell Jake, I'm not comfortable keeping this from him.' The message read. Jake was confused but he continued to read on.

'You know the deal, we don't tell him anything. It was a mistake.' Jane had replied.

'I don't appreciate you solely blaming me either. You're as much to blame as I am.' Reece had put back.

Then, the door opened, and Jane emerged. Jane walked in to see Jake on her phone.

"Jake," She said, panic-stricken, "What are you doing?"

Jake looked up at her, expressionless and void of all emotion. This wasn't good.

"What are these messages about?" Jake asked, passing Jane the phone.

In that moment, time stopped for Jane. She could come clean, or she could maintain the lie. Had she finally been caught?

"It's nothing," Jane said, "What are you even doing looking at my phone?"

Jane tried to twist it round. She started to feel the power and control lurking over her again like what she used against Reece to stop him from telling Jake. After all, Jake couldn't have any other evidence. Then, Jake pulled Jane's pregnancy test from out of his pocket and held it in front of her.

"Wh-," Jane stuttered, struggling to get her words out, "Where did you get that?"

"So, it is yours then." Jake said, seeking confirmation for what he already knew.

Jane nodded, standing in silence. She didn't know what to say. At this point, he'd investigated it more than she thought. Jake put his head down, waiting to hear Jane say the baby was his. She never did. She just stood there, quiet as a mouse. A mouse in a mousetrap which had already given up.

"How could you?" Jake said, "After all we've been through."

Tears started welling up in Jake's eyes. He wanted to cry but he didn't want to give her the satisfaction of thinking she was worth his tears. Jake tried to be as strong as he could. Jane still stood there, silent.

"Reece," Jake shouted, starting to get angry at Jane's lack of empathy, "Of all people?"

Jane went to say something, but she couldn't muster the words. She was heartbroken. She knew this would be the end of her and Jake's relationship. The truth was, as well as being heartbroken, Jane was alleviated in a way. No longer would she have to watch every word she said. No longer would she have to bear the weight on her shoulders of keeping this terrible secret.

"I'm sorry." That was the only thing Jane could say.

"You're sorry?" Jake shouted, throwing the

pregnancy test at the wall causing Jane to flinch, "You sleep with my best friend and all you can say is sorry?"

Jane looked into Jake's eyes, and she was terrified. She hadn't seen this level of anger from Jake before. Jake was filled with rage. Jane went to hug Jake, but he pushed her off him.

"Don't," He said, "Just. Don't."

Jake walked around her as she started to sob. He went straight into the bedroom. Jane heard the unzipping noise of a bag and started to panic. She ran into the room and saw Jake packing.

"What are you doing?" Jane asked Jake as he slammed drawers open, grabbing his clothes and stuffing them into his bag.

"Packing," Jake told her with no emotion in his voice but anger in his eyes, "You better pack your things before we leave."

'We leave.' Clearly, he wasn't going to leave without her. Jane tried to grab Jake to stop him from packing, but he just pushed her off him and carried on. Jane grabbed her bag, trembling and sobbing, and started to put her clothes in there as quickly as she could.

Jake finished packing his clothes and toiletries and started loading up the car with their things. He yanked the towels out of the holders so hard that she was surprised they never came off the wall. Jake didn't care though. He couldn't care about anything anymore. So much for a nice weekend.

"Jake please," Jane tried to plead with Jake as he stormed through the cabin gathering their belongings, "Let me explain."

"What is there to explain?" Jake replied, still gathering items, "Are you going to give me the details?"

"It was a drunken mistake," Jane replied, "You'd stormed off and Reece and I got drunk. One thing led to another, and he came on to me."

Jake stopped dead in his tracks.

"I'd stormed off," Jake turned around, taking a moment to choose his next words, "You're really going to try and shift the blame on to me?"

"No that's no-" Jane tried to correct herself, but she was stopped by Jake mid-sentence.

"I've heard enough," He told her, "Put your stuff in the car."

Jane froze for a moment, still sobbing.

"NOW." Jake shouted at her, pure anger in his voice.

Jane picked up her clothes and her bag which she had just about finished packing. She stuffed the remainder of the clothes into her bag as she paced through the cabin and out to the car. Jake locked the cabin door behind him and got into his car. He reversed off the drive erratically, scaring the life out of Jane. He dropped the key off at the reception on the way out and then took off. Jake wanted to get home as soon as possible.

Jane tried to talk to Jake at various points

throughout the drive back, but he didn't even acknowledge her. Jake wanted this all to be over. It was a long drive back for the both of them. Jane asked if they could stop at the service station, but Jake completely ignored her. She had never seen him like this before. Jake exited the motorway and got to the island where they would usually turn right to go to their house.

"Jake," Jane sheepishly tried to tell Jake he had missed the turn, "Our house is back there."

Jake didn't respond. He just carried on driving. He pulled up outside Reece's house.

"No Jake," She begged, "Whatever you're about to do, don't."

Jake got out of the car and took her bag full of clothes out of the boot. He stormed to Reece's front door, opening the passenger door of his car on the way. Reece opened the door at the sound of shouting and crying coming from Jane.

"Jake?" Reece said, confused by the commotion. Then it clicked for him.

"These are hers," Jake said as he threw the bag at Reece which caused him to stumble back slightly, "Clearly she wants you more than me."

Reece was stunned. 'How did he know? Did Jane tell him?'

Jake stormed back to the car, staring at Jane as she remained seated in the passenger seat.

"Get out," Jake told Jane, unclipping her seat belt, "Now."

Jane sobbed and tried one last time to reason with Jake, but he wasn't having it. Jake lifted her out of the car, dropped her handbag on the floor, and shut the door behind him as he walked around the car. As Jake went to get into the car, he could see the tears welling up in Reece's eyes.

"What the fuck are you crying for?" Jake shouted at Reece, "You've won. Congratulations."

"Ryan's dead, Jake," Reece said through tears, Jane looked over at him, "He was murdered."

Jake paused for a moment, shaking his head in disbelief. He then got into the car, void of emotion, and drove home. Jake sped back home, using his emotions to fuel his driving. He got home and walked in, locking the door behind him. He'd left all the bags from the trip in the boot of the car. Jake felt completely lost. He went into the living room and paused for a moment to think. Out of the corner of his eye, he saw a photograph of him and Jane on their wedding day.

Jake headed over to the picture and picked it up. He looked at it for a moment, shedding a tear which dropped onto the picture. Rage filled Jake once more. He threw the picture at the wall causing the glass on the frame to shatter.

A broken picture of a broken marriage. Jake collapsed to the floor in tears and sobbed for hours on end. He didn't want it to be over, but it was.

10 FATE OF A FRIEND

Jane stormed into Reece's house. Reece shut the door behind her. Tensions were high.

"I swear," Reece told Jane, following her into the kitchen, "I never said a word."

Jane was silent, her hands covering her face.

"You've got to believe me," Reece added, "I didn't tell a soul."

"Shut up Reece," Jane snapped back, "Just for a minute."

Jane was trying to come to terms with what had happened. Reece started to break down. It had only been a few hours since Fred had told him that it was Ryan's body that they had found by the Old Windmill. Reece went straight into the cupboard where he kept his whiskey and poured himself a glass which he drank neat. He then poured himself another. Jane watched as Reece drank himself to despair. Both of them were at a loss.

The rain started to come down heavily as the day went on. Jane was sat on her own in the living room whilst Reece sat drinking in the kitchen. Neither of them knew what to do. Jane had assumed she was homeless, but it was too late to call any of her friends now to ask for somewhere to stay for the night. She should've done it earlier, but she was trying to get over what had transpired. Jane sat watching television but wasn't really paying attention, her mind was elsewhere. Reece walked into the living room with a cup of tea for Jane and handed it to her.

"If you need somewhere to stay tonight, I've got a spare bedroom." Reece told Jane, trying to be supportive.

"Thank you," Jane replied with a smile, "I'll have to take you up on that."

Reece nodded and grabbed her clothing bag from by her feet. He took the bag upstairs and placed it on the bed in the room where she would be sleeping for the night. Reece came back downstairs and offered to cook for Jane, but she refused. She couldn't eat. Her nerves and stress were too much for her to handle.

Jane took herself to bed early but couldn't sleep. Reece stayed up for a while and eventually took himself to bed just after midnight. The next morning Jane woke up early after only a few hours of sleep. Reece was still asleep, trying to sleep off the heavy amount of booze he had consumed the night before.

Jane made herself a drink and sat in the living room for a bit. She had no idea what to do. She sat there for an hour. Her silence was then interrupted by Reece coming down the stairs to get some water.

"Morning," Reece said to her as he made his way towards the kitchen, "Do you want any breakfast?"

"I'm alright thanks Reece." Jane responded. She still couldn't eat, she just sat thinking about Jake. Reece came in and sat in the living room with a glass of water and a bowl of cereal. The two sat there for a while, not saying a word to one another.

"I don't know what to do," Jane opened up the conversation again, "I've never seen Jake like that before."

"I honestly thought he was going to punch me." Reece replied to Jane, eating his cereal.

"I think I'm going to go to the house," Jane told Reece, "See if he's calmed down at all."

"Bad idea," Reece replied with a mouthful of food, "He'll definitely need some more time."

Jane nodded in agreeance but didn't take on board anything Reece had said. She knew Jake and knew right about now he'd be starting to miss her. It would be her perfect chance to speak to him. Jane had all the things she needed for now at Reece's, so she got herself ready and headed out, telling Reece she was going to clear her head. Jane walked for about ten minutes and then called for a local taxi once she was out of range of Reece's house. She gave the destination as Jake's house and off she went.

The taxi dropped Jane off outside. She walked to the front door and put her key in, but it wouldn't unlock. Jake had already changed the locks to the house. Jane banged on the door shouting for Jake, but he never came to the door. She sat on the doorstep and waited for twenty minutes, knocking on the door every four to five minutes. After those twenty minutes had passed, Jake still hadn't come to the door.

She knew he was in as she could see the glare of the television through tilted blinds. Jane knocked once more and then she heard a noise come from the side of the house. Three black bin bags came over the top of the gate one by one and all landed next to her car.

"Jake!" She shouted, clearly knowing he was home now, "Let's talk."

Jake didn't respond, he just slammed the back door of the house behind him. Jane contemplated climbing over the gate until she heard him lock the door. He had no intention of speaking to her. Jane looked into the black bin bags and saw that they were full of her clothes, jewellery, and other belongings. Jane started to tear up, it had to be over now. As she picked up the bin bags, Jane heard another sound. Her car keys had been pushed through the letterbox of the front door.

Jane picked them up and proceeded to put the bin bags into the boot of her car. Eyes filled with tears, she took one last look at the house and saw Jake standing in the bedroom window. His eyes were streaming with tears. Jane slowly waved at him, more like a goodbye than a hello. Jake didn't wave back, he just turned around and walked away. Jane never saw him come to any of the windows after that. She got into her car, started the engine, and reversed off the drive. She drove away without looking back, looking at the house once more would be too painful for her to leave. Years and years of her happiest memories were held between the walls of that house. She had thrown all that away for one night with Reece. One night was all it took to destroy their marriage.

Jane now had to try and find somewhere to live. She didn't want to stay at Reece's because that's where all the problems started. She hadn't got any family to call on, so she called around to various friends to ask for their help. However, none of them could. They all either had no room or they had kids which took priority. Jane was well and truly alone, just like Jake. Not only had her night with Reece destroyed his life, but it had destroyed her own as well. Jane had no choice but to go back to Reece's house. Jane parked the car on the drive and collected the bags out of the boot. Reece opened the door to see her carrying three bags towards the door.

"You went to see him," Reece stated, "Didn't you?"

"Not now Reece." Jane answered, making her way past Reece who was still standing in the doorway. She dropped her bags down in the hallway, clearly out of breath from carrying them.

"Have you found anywhere to stay yet?" Reece asked, shutting the front door, and following Jane as she made her way into the kitchen.

"No, not yet," Jane replied, filling a glass with milk from out of the fridge, "I can't find anywhere."

"Well, you can stop here for as long as you need to," Reece told her, putting his hand on her shoulder, "I could use the company right about now."

Jane smiled, moving Reece's hand from her shoulder. She didn't want to give him any mixed signals. Reece understood and smiled at her. Jane grabbed two of the bin bags and went to take them upstairs, Reece followed her up with the third bin bag.

Jake stayed at home and started drinking to cope with Jane's betrayal. At the same time, he was mourning the loss of Ryan, whose name had now been publicly revealed as the murder victim. The news report read that Ryan was stabbed three times which led to his death. Reading about it took Jake back to when Eric died, someone else who had been a friend of Jake's who passed away. At this point, Jake started to think that he was cursed. Whilst Ryan wasn't necessarily his friend, it still hurt at the fact that he'd been killed in such a horrific way. Plus, the way he learned about Ryan's death was even more tragic. It was horrible to hear about the fate of a friend in any situation, let alone that one.

Over the next few days, Ryan's family arranged his

funeral. They set a date which they announced on Ryan's social media pages for all his friends to see. Wednesday the nineteenth of July. One o'clock in the afternoon. Jake contemplated going but he couldn't bring himself to do it. On the day of the funeral, he parked just outside the cemetery so he could see the hearse take Ryan's coffin into the crematorium for the service.

Jake looked around and saw Reece standing with Jane who was there supporting him. Jake got filled with anger. She cared so little about him that she just ran straight into Reece's arms. Even more than that, Jake felt like Reece had no respect for him. Jake decided that it wasn't the time or place to make a scene, so he started his car and drove away.

Jake didn't know that Jane and Reece were only friends at this point. The funeral had been left open so anyone could attend to pay their respects. Reece had asked Jane to go for support as he was to be one of the four coffin bearers. The other three being Fred, Olly, and Jason. Jane had felt a bit awkward being at the funeral. She didn't know Ryan all too well and had only met him a couple of times.

After the service, they all gathered at the Fradley's Arms in memory of Ryan. It was hard for everyone to say goodbye to Ryan though, especially with his killer still being unknown to the Police and at large.

"Who could do such a thing?" Fred asked, looking over at the picture of Ryan on the table.

"I hope I never meet them," Olly said in response,

"Whoever did it will be fucking dead."

Olly swore revenge on Ryan's killer, thinking he was some sort of vigilante. The police hadn't even come close to identifying a murder suspect yet, as the killer was smart and had covered their tracks. Jane was shocked by Reece's lack of words and could clearly see he was emotional. He tried hard to stay sober for the funeral and the wake afterwards, whilst he usually got drunk to forget, he actually wanted to remember Ryan's service.

Reece and Jane got home at about six o'clock in the evening after they stopped off for food on the way home. Jane took her coat off and hung it up on the door. Reece walked into the kitchen, still holding the order of service from Ryan's funeral. He then put it on the fridge and placed a magnet over it to make sure it wouldn't fall. Reece stood for a moment and stared at the fridge, a tear slowly falling from his eye and down his cheek. Jane put her arm around him to comfort him.

Reece moved away from Jane and walked into the living room where he took a seat on the sofa. He was clearly agitated about the funeral, so Jane left him to it. Jane took herself upstairs and watched television in bed. Shortly after, Reece came into her room and lay next to her. Jane muted the TV.

"So," Reece said, "What next?"

"What do you mean?" Jane replied, confused by Reece's entrance.

"Didn't you see Jake there today?" Reece asked

her, "His car was parked up at the entrance."

"Your point being?" Jane quizzed Reece about what he was trying to say.

"He'll have seen us together. We both know what he's going to assume," Reece explained, "It's only a matter of time until he's back in touch to vent his anger again."

"Let him," Jane replied, "We're only living together, we're not exactly dating."

Reece got up from the bed and walked to the door.

"I've just got a bad feeling that he's going to be angry." Reece replied, walking out of the bedroom, and shutting the door. Jane lay there for a moment and then unmuted the TV. 'Surely Jake wouldn't be that angry still? He never stays angry for long about anything,' Jane thought to herself. Jane eventually turned the TV off and lay down, dropping off to sleep.

Jake wouldn't sleep that night though, tossing and turning. He eventually got up and started looking at divorce procedures and what he would need to do to get a divorce from Jane. Neither he nor Jane had got the strength to declare that they wanted to get a divorce. Jake knew that it was time though. He needed it so he could move on, and he also thought that Jane would need it so that she could move on. Even if that was with Reece.

Jake went online and booked an appointment with a solicitor to get a divorce petition written up. Jake booked his appointment for a few days away. He wanted to get it dealt with as soon as possible. He had some time off work, after calling in sick for the week. Jake drove to the solicitors office on the day of the appointment and sat down with his solicitor. He briefly explained the situation. It hurt too much for him to go into the details about what happened. Jake got his divorce from Jane in motion. It would take a while for the papers to be sent off though, so Jake had to wait.

Jane and Reece slowly grew closer, despite the obvious issues in their relationship, they had a bond which started to grow more and more. They both knew that there was something there that pointed to them being more than just friends, but neither of them wanted to admit it to the other. They went out for meals and did all sorts of things together, just as good friends would. They started to be happier and enjoy each other's company. Jane didn't actively look for somewhere new to live, she was quite happy staying with Reece for a while longer. The stronger their friendship, the happier they made each other. Jane stopped Reece feeling lonely, and Reece stopped Jane feeling lonely.

Around the middle of the week, whilst out for the day with Reece, Jane received a text from Jake. She didn't open it at first and never told Reece that he had texted her. She tried her best to avoid it. She was frightened that Jake's text would be him venting his frustration at her about her newfound bond with

Reece. After all, Reece had warned her that Jake would likely be in touch.

She dreaded to think what the message said, so at the end of the day, she went to sleep having not opened it.

11 DOUBLE WHAMMY

Jane woke up the next morning and checked the time on her phone. Five minutes past eight. Jake's message was still there, unopened. Jane continued to ignore it. She got out of bed, had a wash, and got ready for her day. She had the house to herself today. Reece had started back at work after being allowed bereavement leave due to Ryan dying. The company he worked for were really generous to him, letting him have the time off.

Jane decided that she was going to do some cleaning around the house, to try and keep her mind off the fact that Jake had messaged her. Jane kept busy for hours on end. Before she even knew it, it was half past eleven. Jane sat down with a cup of tea and picked up her phone which she had left in the living room whilst she did the housework. 'Message from Jake' was still at the top of her notifications bar. Jane paused for a moment and then decided to open it.

'Hey, hope you're well. Can we meet? x' Jake never put kisses on texts, so this was out of character for him. They had spent some time away from each other. Maybe he did genuinely want to meet. Jane certainly hoped so, she was relieved to see that Jake had texted her, but didn't want to tell Reece. This would be something which she would have to do on her own. Jane texted him back.

'Hey, yeah. Do you want to do lunch?' Jane replied. She left out any kisses to see if he put them again. Then she would know that something was definitely wrong. Minutes later, Jake texted her back. 'Great, meet at Ellen's café? x.' Another kiss, something was wrong. There was no doubt what this could be other than bad news. Jane texted Jake back 'See you at one.' She didn't get another response then from Jake and just planned on getting ready for meeting him.

Jake was delighted to see that Jane had agreed to meet him. Jake wanted to see if she still loved him and if she would fight for their relationship. He'd had some time to think about it and, whilst he could never forgive her for cheating, he could at least try to make the relationship work. He thought about how lonely and empty he felt without Jane, and how he still loved her, and desperately wanted to save the broken pieces that remained of their marriage.

Jane was getting ready to leave when she got a call from Reece.

"Hey, I've got lunch off," Reece told her, "Do want to come meet me for food?"

Jane knew she had plans with Jake but didn't want to share that with Reece. Plus, she had no reasonable excuse to give to Reece given that he knew she wasn't supposed to be doing anything all day.

"Sure, I'll come to your work." She replied. As long as she didn't spend too long with Reece, she could make lunch with Reece and then just get a drink with Jake instead. Jane locked the house up and left to meet Reece. They met on the car park at his workplace at quarter past twelve and walked to a local pub where they grabbed a sandwich each. Time flew by.

On the way to the café, Jake went to the local florist and bought some flowers which he planned on giving to Jane. Jake put these in the car with him and made his way to Ellen's café early. He got there at quarter to one but couldn't see Jane. Jake waited until one o'clock and just assumed she was running behind. He didn't bother texting her as he wanted to see if he could trust her. By quarter past one, Jake got fed up of waiting. He dumped the flowers into a nearby bin and left. There was no chance for them now. Jake was eager to get the divorce put through.

"Oh," Reece said, looking at his watch, "It's ten past one, I best be getting back."

"It is?" Jane replied, jumping to her feet, "Surely

not!"

"Why the mad rush?" Reece asked, "I'm the one that's going to be late."

"I have an appointment that's all," Jane responded, "I'll see you at home."

Jane caught a taxi and rushed to the café, completely forgetting her car was at Reece's work. 'It'll be okay there,' she thought to herself. Jane got to the café at twenty-five minutes past one, but there was no sign of Jake. She saw some flowers poking out of a nearby bin with a name tag hanging off of them.

It read 'To Jane, From Jake x.' Jane instantly got her phone out and called Jake, but the call went straight to the answer tone. She left a voicemail.

"Jake, it's me. I'm sorry, can you please call me when you get this?" She said into the answer message. 'Maybe Jake was trying to make repairs and I just blown it,' she thought to herself. Jane headed back to Reece's work and picked up her car. The first place she stopped at was Jake's. She saw his car on the drive, so she knew he was home. Jane knocked frantically on the door. She saw a shadow slowly approach and unlock the door. It was Jake. He didn't say anything when he unlocked the door. He just stared her in the face. The look in his eyes was one of loneliness. Despair. The one emotion she couldn't see in him was love.

"Jake," Jane opened with, "I'm so sorry. I was out and I just lost track of the time. I didn't mean to miss it."

"It's done with now," Jake replied in a monotone voice, void of any emotion, "Keep an eye on your post. My solicitors are sending the divorce petition through. Keep an eye out."

Jake turned around and went to shut the door on Jane, but she put her foot in the door.

"The what?" Jane panicked. She never expected that Jake would actually be willing to divorce her. She felt that it was over, but she honestly wanted to believe they would get through this.

"You heard me." Jake responded, putting his head down and pushing the door again. This caused Jane's foot to get shifted backwards. She was in shock. All those years. Gone. Not knowing what to do with herself, Jane left to go back to Reece's. It seemed that his home would also be hers for a while longer.

Jake watched on through the living room window, observing Jane's car drive off into the distance. He knew it was over. Jake screamed in rage and punched the wall, causing his fist to go through it, leaving a hand-sized hole in the wall. Jake caught his breath and pulled his arm out of the wall. It was covered in white dust. Jake looked down at his hand and slowly saw bits of blood emerge from his knuckles. When he had put his hand through the wall, he had made a few minor cuts.

Jake headed over to the kitchen sink and washed the dust and the blood off. Jake's temper was getting worse. He was losing his grip. Jake wrapped his hand up and headed over to the kitchen where he opened a bottle of Scotch. Just when he was about to pour it, he stopped to think. 'Was this really the path he wanted to go down?' After a brief pause, Jake poured himself a drink and downed it neat. Three o'clock in the afternoon and he was already drinking. He was just glad that Jane didn't see him like this.

Jane drove straight home after going to Jake's and started to get overwhelmed with emotion. She got in and cried her eyes out for two straight hours. She stopped crying shortly before Reece got home. She dried her tears away to stop Reece from finding out she had been crying. He would only ask why she was upset which would lead to her breaking down even more.

Reece got in and could tell that something was wrong with Jane, but she wouldn't reveal what it was that she was upset about. To cheer her up, Reece convinced Jane to go to the Fradley's arms with him. Reece was set to be meeting with Fred, Olly, and Jason. Jane liked seeing them, so she agreed to tag along. The group were aware of what was going on between Reece and Jane, so they weren't surprised when she turned up at the pub on the evening.

"How's it going guys?" Reece asked, walking over to the table where Fred, Olly and Jason were already situated, "You remember Jane don't you?"

Jane gave a short but sweet wave.

"Yeah of course we do," Fred replied, polite as always, "How are you?"

"I've seen better days," Jane answered, "How

about yourself?"

"Not enough people ask that," Fred pointed out, "But I'm very well. Thank you so much for asking."

Fred looked over at Jason and glared. Reece and Jane were confused, wondering what it was that Fred meant by the strange comment.

"Are we missing something?" Reece asked nervously. He found Fred's behaviour rather odd given that by this time, it was only eight in the evening and Fred was driving, so he wouldn't be drunk.

"Fred just pointed out that when Jason comes over to the table, he buys his own drink and never asks anyone how they are," Olly interrupted, "And now he won't let it go."

Reece and Jane both laughed, finding the pettiness of it all humorous. The group all had a few drinks, except for Fred and Olly who were driving. Tonight was their race night where they raced each other up and down a local strip. No cameras, no Police, and no other boy racers. It was their little spot they used to go to on the last Thursday of every month.

"Have any of you heard anything from the Police about the investigation?" Jane asked, presumably on about Ryan. All of those present shook their heads. Reece looked down at the floor.

"I do miss him," Jason said, raising his glass, "To Ryan!"

"To Ryan!" Fred and Olly said simultaneously. Jane raised her glass too, but Reece continued to stare at the floor.

"To Ryan." Reece said, finally raising his glass. Something bothered him, but the others couldn't point out what it was.

They stayed at the pub until closing time. The bell rang to announce they were closing, and they all left. Fred and Olly got into their cars.

"Last one there is a rotten egg." Fred challenged Olly as he got into his car.

"A bit like your car then." Olly replied, winking at Fred, and getting into his car.

Fred's car was a two-thousand and eleven Nissan 350z. Silver in colour, with black wheels. Olly's car was a nineteen-ninety-six Mitsubishi Eclipse GST which he had painted in black, with blacked-out windows and black wheels. He loved it more than life itself. Both were beautifully sounding cars. Pumping out harmful fumes that smelt too good to resist. They both revved their engines at each other for a moment, trying to show off in front of Jason, Reece, and Jane. They then took off into the night. Jason said his farewells and left Jane and Reece to make their way home. They got in and went straight up to bed. They both told each other 'goodnight' and then shut their doors.

Jane woke up in the early hours of the morning to hear Reece talking on the phone. He sounded panicked. She rolled over to check her phone. The time read four-fifty-two.

"Calm down," Jane heard Reece frantically tell the

person on the other end of the phone, "I'm on the way."

Jane put on her dressing gown and went into Reece's room to see him standing with his hands on his head.

"What's happened Reece?" She asked, instantly being able to tell something was wrong.

"I need to get to the hospital." Reece told Jane. He put a tee shirt and jeans on and went to head straight out.

"Hang on I'm coming with you," Jane replied, starting to panic, "What's happened?"

"Get some clothes on," He told her, "I've got no time to explain now."

Jane rushed to put some clothes on. She didn't have time to do her hair. Instead, she grabbed a hair bobble and a packet of mints which she ate on the way. Reece didn't say anything, he just drove as if his life depended on it. Or someone else's.

They arrived at the accident and emergency department and saw Jason in the waiting room. He took them through to the ward where Reece saw Olly lying in the bed, covered in casts.

"They found him in his car after having an accident," Jason said, hand over his mouth, clearly emotional, "He was already unresponsive when Police and Ambulance arrived."

"Have you called Fred?" Reece asked. Jason's head dropped. Reece could tell instantly it was going to be bad news, "No. Don't say it."

"I'm sorry Reece," Jason said as he was bought to tears, "The car he hit was Fred's. He was dead on arrival."

Reece collapsed to the floor, breaking down into tears. Jane was in shock. She dropped straight to the floor to comfort him. Reece had already lost Ryan, now he had to go through losing Fred too.

"Why is this happening?" Reece cried out.

"Look," Jason said, sitting next to Reece who at this point was sitting himself back up, "Olly doesn't know about Fred. We've got to be strong for him. You know what Fred meant to him. They were like brothers."

"We're all brothers." Reece replied, wiping his tears away.

Reece got back to his feet with the help of Jane and Jason. They slowly entered the room and sat with Olly who was still unconscious. His partner was there as well. She was the one who called Jason who then called Reece. Olly had been through various surgeries to try and help him. They sat in the room with Olly, seeing nurse after nurse come in to check on his condition. At midday, he slowly opened his eyes as much as he could.

"What happened?" Were the first words out of his mouth, followed by, "Where am I?"

"You had a crash Olly," Jason told him, "You're in the hospital."

"Fred," Olly muttered, "Where's Fred?"

Neither of them knew what to say. They didn't

want to lie and say that Fred was fine, but at the same time, they had no clue how to break the news to him that his best friend was dead. This was going to be a double whammy for Olly. Who would deliver it though? Just then, Jane put her hand on Olly's which was mostly covered by his cast.

"I'm so sorry Olly," She said softly, "Fred didn't make it."

Reece sniffled, trying to stay strong and hold back his tears. Olly glanced at the different people surrounding him in the room, trying to gauge their facial expressions. He didn't want to believe Jane but slowly, the harsh reality started to set in.

"No," He said, "You're lying."

Jane sat in silence. Nobody knew what to say.

"One of you tell me she's lying," Olly cried out, "Tell me I didn't kill Fred."

"It wasn't your fault," Jason said, "It was an accident."

Tears streamed down Olly's face. Tears of guilt. They all felt what Olly was going through. Despite having lost two of their brothers, they were still a family. They needed to stick together.

They all stayed at the hospital, together, for the rest of the day.

Jake

For the third day in a row, Jake didn't bother going into work. He was suffering from a really heavy hangover, which he nursed with more alcohol. He got a call from his boss which he declined at first. At about lunchtime, he got another call which he finally answered.

"Just where the hell are you?" Jake's boss asked.

"Home," Jake replied, "I'm not feeling too well I can't make it in again today."

"Jake, I know you've been going through a lot," His boss told him over the phone, "I can't keep letting you off though, it's not fair on the rest of the team."

"If you're going to sack me just do it already." Jake replied, clearly having lost all hope.

"You've been drinking again, haven't you?" His boss asked him. Jake's bedside table was filled with empty bottles of beer. Some from last night, some from the night before. He wasn't quite sure when each particular one was from. He just knew they were empty.

"What's it to you?" Jake responded to his boss arrogantly.

"Jake, I'm just trying to look out for you," The boss replied, "I can't help you though if you won't give me any details."

"I'm completely fine," Jake told his boss, "I just can't make it today."

Jake's boss could tell that he was hungover. He was still slurring his words, and his demeanour had completely changed from the Jake he once knew.

"My hands are tied Jake," His boss said, "I'm going to have to let you go."

"Well, you can't let me go because I quit." Jake hung up the call with that line and launched his phone at the wall, causing the screen to crack. He didn't really care, he'd got past that point. His life was ruined. All thanks to Reece.

Reece, Jane, and Jason visited Olly as much as they could at the hospital. He was in for a week and got out on Wednesday the second of August. The same day which Jake had been sacked from his job. He got out in time for Fred's funeral which was going to be two days later, however, he was stuck in a wheelchair for the moment. The day of the funeral came around, Reece and Jason were two of Fred's coffin bearers, whilst Fred's father and brother were the other ones who carried his coffin in. They sat through the service and then all gathered for the wake afterwards. However, Olly was notably missing. It was understandable really with his injuries. More than that, he was eaten up by guilt every second of the funeral. He kept seeing the accident play over and over in his head.

"First Ryan and now Fred," Jason said to Reece, "It's fucking unbelievable."

"Don't even start me," Reece replied, "I hadn't been to many funerals before, in the past month I've been to two."

The wounds hadn't quite healed from Ryan's death. His killer still hadn't been found and the Police weren't any closer to naming any suspects. At this point, they had started to accept that Ryan's killer would never be found. They gave a 'cheers' to Ryan and Fred this time. They would both live on in their hearts.

Jane and Reece went home. Reece wanted to start drinking but Jane managed to somehow talk him out of it. Once again, she was supporting him through his tough times. Reece put Fred's order of service on the fridge next to Ryan's, keeping them both together. The pair of them went to bed and got some sleep.

The next morning, Reece woke up and headed downstairs to Jane who was already up and cooking breakfast for them both. Reece was still hurting from losing Fred, and the funeral had bought those memories back up. He tried so hard not to drink, and Jane helped him not to as well. They were halfway into their day when there was a knock at the front door. It was Jason.

"Hey Jase," Reece said, moving beside the door to invite Jason in, "Come on in mate."

Jason kept his head down and didn't say a word. He entered the kitchen and saw Jane in there cooking breakfast. Jane stopped to look at Jason, who went and looked at the orders of service on the fridge.

"It's been tough mate," Reece told Jason, putting his hand on his shoulder, "We'll find a way though."

"Olly's dead." Jason replied. Reece nearly threw up.

"What?" Jane replied, turning round to face Jason.

"He left after the funeral yesterday and his partner said something seemed off with him. He'd told her how he just kept seeing the accident. Last night it got too much for him." Jason explained. Reece sat down on the chair. He wanted to cry but he couldn't seem to form the tears. He'd already used up so many of them on Ryan and Fred.

"When does it end?" Reece stated with his head in his hands.

"She's planning the funeral for next week. I've spoken to her already," Jason told them, "She wants to try and get Olly buried in the plot next to Fred. They were inseparable in life, so she wants them to be the same in death."

The house fell into a deafening silence. Three of them were dead now. Reece couldn't cope with it. When Jason left, Reece went straight for a bottle. Jane tried to stop him, but Reece was determined to drink. Frightened by his commitment to the bottle, Jane let him carry on.

Olly's funeral was on Thursday the tenth of August, just six days after Fred's. Reece didn't want to be a coffin bearer this time. He didn't even go to the wake after the funeral. He showed up for the funeral and left straight after. He couldn't bear to sit through another one so soon after Ryan and Fred's. On that night, Reece was at the lowest point of his life. In a desperate bid to get it to end, Reece attempted suicide. Jane was in the house, upstairs, cleaning up her drawers in her room when she heard the smash of a glass bottle.

Jane rushed down the stairs to find Reece standing

in the kitchen holding a knife to his wrist.

"REECE!" Jane desperately shouted, her voice cracking, "WHAT THE FUCK ARE YOU DOING?"

"I can't take it anymore Jane," Reece shouted back, tears streaming down his face, "I can't take another loss."

"You can't do this Reece," Jane pleaded with him, tears welling up in her eyes, "Please, I beg you."

"What do I have to live for Jane?" Reece shouted back at her, his voice showing he was desperate for an answer to the question, "I've lost nearly everyone I love."

"Us, Reece," She replied, resting her hand on her stomach. Reece lowered the knife before dropping it on the floor.

"I'm pregnant."

12 LOOKING UP

"You're pregnant?" Reece asked Jane, in complete shock.

"Yes," Jane smiled with tears in her eyes, "It's your baby."

Reece was stunned. He took a double take and couldn't believe what he was hearing.

"How do you know it's mine?" Reece questioned Jane, not sure whether to believe her.

"Jake can't have children," She replied, "And I started getting signs not long after we slept together."

Reece was shocked by the news. The tears he initially shed in loss and despair turned to tears of joy and happiness. Once again, he was going to be a dad. Reece went and took a seat in the living room. Jane followed him in and sat down next to him.

"Did Jake know you were pregnant?" Reece asked

Jane, looking over at her.

"He figured it out, that's how he knew I'd cheated on him." Jane responded, looking down at the floor, still ashamed by how it ended with Jake. Deep down, she still had feelings for him. Reece went quiet for a minute and then went into the kitchen to grab his phone.

Whilst in the kitchen, he saw the knife which he had planned on ending his life with mere moments ago. That idea was out the window now. Now he had something to live for. Now, things could start looking up for him.

He picked the knife up, looking at his reflection in the blade before putting it back into the drawer. He then grabbed his phone and went back into the living room where Jane was still sitting. Reece used his phone to book onto an Alcoholic's Awareness course.

"Done." He said, locking his phone and putting it on the fireplace next to the sofa where he was sat. Jane looked over at him, puzzled.

"Done what?" She replied, with a look of slight confusion on her face.

"I've booked onto an alcoholic's awareness course," Reece told Jane, "I'm going to be there for you and for our child."

"I may not feel ready now, but I will be." Reece added, much to Jane's joy.

She smiled and jumped at Reece, giving him a tight hug. Reece hugged her back. An unfamiliar feeling swooped over both of them. A feeling that they both recognised from the night they spent together. A warm feeling. A feeling of love. Jane let go of Reece and they both looked at each other for a moment. Simultaneously, the pair leaned towards each other and shared a kiss. This one felt more than right. This time, Jane wasn't cheating, and Reece wasn't betraying his friend. There was nothing in their way anymore. They could finally be in love.

Reece started his fight against alcohol and attended the meetings to help with his battle. At the same time, he entered into a relationship with Jane. Jane knew from the start that it was right. She never questioned it at all. That feeling was mutually shared. She did sometimes think about Jake, and how she could have handled it better, but she had no doubt in her mind that she had found the right person with Reece. The two could finally admit that they loved each other.

Jake

Jake spent most of his time after losing his job drinking. He had tried to quit a few times, but the bottle always called him back. Jake never saw much of anybody. He only left the house to get necessities, one of those being alcohol. Lots of it.

A couple of neighbours came around to his house to check on him. They knew Jane had left as they had seen the commotion in the street when he threw the bin bags over the gate. Jake would never answer the door to the neighbours though, or anyone for that matter.

His old boss even visited one day to check on his welfare. He had expected that Jake would have asked for his job back by now or at least explained his situation, but Jake never bothered making contact.

Jake watched on as people came and left. With every knock he thought about going to answer the door. In the end, he never did. It was nothing personal. He just didn't want to talk to anyone.

Jake was at the lowest point of his entire life. Guilt from mistakes he had made, despair from losing Jane, and loneliness from isolating himself. These were all the emotions that Jake was being put through on a daily basis. For so long he had tried to be strong but now he was weak.

Jane and Reece

The following few months passed quickly for Jane and Reece but passed at a tremendously slow rate for Jake. Reece slowly was starting to overcome years of alcohol abuse whilst Jake was just starting his. Jane and Reece went out on various dates and took spontaneous trips away. Reece was finally getting back to himself, and he loved it. He loved Jane.

One weekend, Reece decided to take Jane away to the seaside. He had big plans for that weekend. They got up early in the morning and took a drive down, cruising nicely on the motorway. Altogether, with no stops for toilet or refreshment breaks, the journey lasted about two and a half hours.

Once they arrived, they got breakfast at a local

pub. They walked around for a while, admiring the view, before checking into their hotel at mid-day. They spent the day unpacking and going out for a while to do some shopping. Reece had something special planned for their evening. Jane had no clue what he had in store for her. All he told her was that they were going out.

Reece knew this fancy restaurant which he planned on taking Jane to. She was around seventeen weeks pregnant at this point and was just starting her second trimester. Jane was loving her pregnancy, but she was hating the lack of options when it came to clothing. She put on some smart casual clothes. She couldn't fit into her dresses due to the fact that they were all skin-tight and she had started to get bigger.

Jane and Reece made their way down to the restaurant and had a lovely meal. The restaurant was an expensive one, but Reece covered the bill. Jane had started to earn her own money now working in a local shop. However, whatever money she earned went straight into her savings. They had to start preparing for the incoming bills they knew they'd be having once the baby was born. Reece had a lot more disposable income now thanks to giving up drinking. This baby had saved both of their lives and put them on the right track going forwards.

Once they finished their meals, Jane and Reece headed out for a nice walk down the seafront. They stopped in a lovely space and watched the tide moving in and out. It was beautiful.

Jane was pointing something out to Reece, but he wasn't listening to her. Instead, he moved behind her and got down on one knee and waited patiently. Jane turned around to check if Reece was listening and was in complete shock by what she saw before her eyes.

"Jane," Reece said, trying not to mess up the words. He'd planned this out in his head. Weeks of rehearsing in front of the bathroom mirror had led to this moment, "For the past few months, you've made me as happy as I can be. You and this baby have both been my saviour. If it wasn't for you both, I'd be dead."

Jane's eyes welled up with tears of happiness as she put both of her hands over her mouth. She wanted to shout her answer already, but she had to try and be patient.

"So now I ask. Will you marry me?" Reece asked as he started to get nervous.

"YES!" Jane shouted at the top of her voice. Reece smiled as relief washed over him. Jane gave him the biggest possible hug that she could, holding him tight and never wanting to let go. There were a few people around who could see what was going on and clapped for them. No one could be as happy as they were in that moment. Reece slid the diamond-encrusted ring onto her finger and kissed her.

They stayed in that spot for the next hour and a half. Jane didn't want to move as she didn't want the moment to end. Eventually, they had to move on. It was getting late, and they both wanted to get back to the hotel.

Before they went into their room, they headed down to the bar. Reece ordered them both fizzy drinks which were on draught. Jane couldn't drink because of the baby and Reece wouldn't drink. A true showing of his commitment to Jane and their baby. Alcohol hadn't touched Reece's lips at this point for two months. An achievement in which he was proud of.

They both returned to the room and lay on the bed together. Jane admired her new engagement ring. She couldn't stop smiling. She was moving it in and out of the light, watching as the diamond glistened. It must have cost Reece a fortune.

"It's beautiful." Jane said through the biggest smile Reece had ever seen. She held her hand in the air for them both to see the ring. Reece didn't say anything, he just smiled at her.

"I love you." Reece told Jane. It wasn't the first time he had said it, and it wouldn't be the last.

"I love you too." Jane replied.

The two went to bed not long after that. A date that they could cherish in their hearts for a long time. Saturday the twenty-first of October. The date they got engaged. The date they realised that everything in their lives was starting to take shape.

They didn't announce their engagement straight away. They wanted to get everything organised first. Plus, Jane's ultrasound scan was coming up in that same week.

Jane and Reece went together for the scan. They were given the option of knowing the gender of the baby early if they wanted to. They'd already thought about it, and both decided that they didn't want to know. Instead, they wanted it to be a surprise on the big day.

Once the ultrasound had passed, a week after they had got engaged, they organised their engagement party. Jane put the post online, eager to announce their news.

Jake

At the time for Jake, it would just be another day. He'd got himself a new routine by this point. He'd wake up sometime between nine o'clock and eleven o'clock, clean his teeth, possibly have a shower, open a beer whilst watching the TV, and then go back to bed if he could make it up the stairs on the evening. The only time his routine changed was if he ran out of beer. In which case he would have to go to the shop and buy some more.

It was a sad life for him. He kept on living it though. The thought that one day Jane may be back in touch with him kept him going. He knew it was over though. The divorce process was well over halfway at this point. 'The downfall of a successful journalist.' Now that would be a good headline.

On Saturday the twenty-eighth of October, at two o'clock in the afternoon, Jake got a notification pop-up on his phone. With a half-empty bottle of beer in one hand, and his phone in the other, he opened the notification.

'Jane and Reece would like to announce their engagement. Party on Sunday the Fifth of November at their house. Starting at one o'clock in the afternoon and finishing at five o'clock in the evening.'

Jake looked at the post and a feeling of drunken anger washed over him. Jake launched the bottle at the wall, causing it to smash and spill beer down the wall. The more he had been drinking, the worse his temper was getting. Jake sprung to his feet and went to grab his car keys. Enough. He was going to confront Reece and win Jane back. Jake got into his car and started the engine. He put the car in reverse, only to stop himself from pulling off the drive. Jake had a change of heart. He wasn't going to accomplish anything by going over there and yelling at them. He needed to play it smart. Jake wanted to hurt Reece so badly that he wouldn't recover. He had just the plan.

Now was the time that he put his plan into action. 'It's all in the name of love. So it's all justified.'

The day soon rolled around. Jane and Reece prepared the house beautifully for the party. Ribbons hung from the ceiling. Flowers placed in a range of different vases sat throughout the house to spruce it up.

Slowly, guests started arriving. They were expecting somewhere between twenty and thirty guests to arrive. By half past two in the afternoon, the majority of the anticipated guests had arrived and were enjoying the light buffet which Jane had put on.

Jake decided to go to the party. He dressed up nicely, sporting a polo shirt and jeans. He had been drinking, so he arranged for a taxi to take him there. He downed one more 'good luck' beer as he was calling them now, and then left the house when the taxi parked up outside. Jake arrived in no time and knocked on the door. Jane answered.

"Jake," She said in shock, she had never expected him to turn up, "What a surprise."

Reece heard Jake's name and came straight over to the door. A couple of guests who were within earshot heard his name and went silent.

"Can I come in?" Jake asked, holding two gift bags, one in either hand.

"Of course." Reece told Jake, outstretching his arm, and welcoming him into the house. Jake walked straight past them and entered the house.

"What is he doing here?" Jane whispered to Reece.

"I don't know," He replied, "You put out the invites."

Jake turned around. Jane and Reece stood upright and smiled at Jake. Jake pretended that he didn't hear them whispering about him.

"Nothing here's changed I see," Jake said, looking around, "I got you both a gift each."

Jake stretched his arms out to pass them both the gifts. Jane could smell the alcohol coming off Jake. It was a potent smell. Horrid.

Reece smiled and accepted Jake's gift. Jane

followed suit. As she took the gift, he gently took hold of her hand. Reece watched Jake like a hawk.

"Is that the ring?" Jake asked, "It looks beautiful!"

Jane smiled and moved her hand away. Reece focused his concentration back on opening his gift. Jake looked over at Reece, wanting to capture his reaction. Reece pulled the gift out of the bag. A bottle of Whiskey, an expensive one at that.

"Thanks Jake," Reece was stunned for words, "I've actually given up drinking though now."

"That's brilliant news," Jake replied, smiling at Reece, "Keep it anyways. You never know when you'll need it."

Jake winked at Reece as he said that. He then proceeded to look over at Jane, waiting for her to open his gift to her. Jane put her hand into the bag and pulled out a statue. The statue was of a man and a pregnant woman. The man had his one hand on the pregnant lady's stomach and his other hand around her. The woman was in some sort of dress. Jane examined the model and noticed it had a chip in the corner.

"Sorry about that," Jake said as he saw Jane rub her finger over the chip, "It dropped it when I got home. The store wouldn't let me swap it for another."

"It's lovely Jake," She responded, smiling at him, "I wouldn't change it."

Jake smiled back at her and then over at Reece who smiled back.

"I want to apologise. To both of you," Jake told

them, consciously scratching his nose, "The way I've reacted and treated you both recently has been appalling. I'm sorry for any stress I've put you through."

Reece and Jane were both shocked by his apology. It was one of the last things they expected.

"Thank you, Jake," Reece said, shaking Jake's hand, "It means a lot."

Jake smiled at them once more and then head over to the buffet table, grabbed a paper plate, and started to eat. People were staying away from Jake because of the powerful odour of alcohol reeking from him. Jake had noticed what they were doing, but he didn't really care. Jake walked around the kitchen and saw the orders of service on the fridge for Ryan, Fred, and Olly. Reece walked over to Jake.

"I bet you never heard about Fred and Olly, did you?" Reece asked Jake. Jake stared for a minute and then snapped into focus.

"No," He replied, "What happened?"

"Car accident," Reece said, Jake looked over at Reece, shocked, "They were racing on Corbett Road like they always used to, and Olly's brakes failed. He hit Fred and killed him."

"Shit," Jake replied, taking a swig of a bottle of beer he had bought with him, "That's horrible. They were best mates."

"I know," Reece agreed, "Olly couldn't cope with the guilt and ended up killing himself."

Jake shook his head.

"It's a shame," Jake said to Reece, "They were good lads."

Jake and Reece clanged glasses and Jake finished his beer.

"I best be leaving anyways," Jake told Reece as Jane come over, "Things to do."

"Are you still working for the paper?" Reece asked, "I haven't seen your name under any headlines in a while."

"Oh no, I'm not," Jake replied, "I got sacked."

Reece and Jane were stunned.

"Anyways," Jake said, giving both of them hugs and sharing his intoxicating smell with them, "I'll see you around."

Jake turned around and went straight for the door. He didn't look back, he just shut the door behind him and walked down the street. Once he was out of view, he called a taxi to take him home.

Jane and Reece were in shock as they watched Jake leave through the window. A completely unexpected visit from Jake. Not to mention that he was surprisingly nice to them both given what had happened between the three of them. They both had mixed feelings about the whole interaction.

For Jake, the party couldn't have gone any better.

13 HEADS OR TAILS

Jane and Reece were packing up after the party. There was rubbish everywhere. Cans and bottles covered most of the tables throughout the living room and kitchen. There were paper plates throughout the house. It took them ages to clean up. It was worth it though, they had a good time. Once they finished tidying up, they started putting any gifts they had received into the appropriate areas. Reece put the bottle of Whiskey that Jake bought him in a cupboard which he then locked. He would feel bad for getting rid of the bottle, as he saw it as a peace offering from Jake. At the same time, he couldn't drink it for obvious reasons. Jane put the statue in the living room. It looked beautiful on the windowsill.

After everything was sorted, they ordered a takeaway from a local Indian restaurant and put a film on. They cuddled up on the sofa until ten o'clock in the evening when they went to bed. At this point, they were sharing a bedroom. The two of them lay next to each other in bed.

"It was a surprise to see Jake today." Jane said to Reece as he read his book.

"For sure," He replied, "I expected him to try and cause a scene."

Jane nodded. "He looked a bit rough though didn't he?"

"He did," Reece agreed, looking over at Jane, "It's a shame for him."

"Could you smell the alcohol on him?" Jane asked, clearly concerned about Jake.

"I could," Reece told her as he looked back at his book, "He'd obviously been drinking."

"He needs help Reece," Jane stated, causing Reece to look over at her again, "He's obviously struggling."

"It's nothing he can't handle," Reece disagreed with Jane, "He's a strong lad."

A moment of silence fell between the two of them. They hadn't had many disagreements since getting together, but this was clearly going to be a big one. Jane still cared for Jake. After all, she had been married to him for years. Her priority was Reece now though, so she didn't say anything else on the matter.

"Goodnight," Jane said to Reece, "See you in the morning."

They shared a kiss and then both went to sleep. Jane took slightly longer to sleep, she was being eaten up by guilt. She felt responsible for Jake's downfall.

For the next few days, they both carried on as normal. Both of them went to work, did their hours, and returned home. They stayed in on the nights, often watching movies or planning for the baby.

Jake, on the other hand, started trying to cut back on his drinking. His plan was in motion now, and he needed to be ready for when the inevitable next step came into play. He knew Jane well. He knew that turning up at their house reeking of alcohol and clearly being under the influence would cause her concern. Now, all he had to do was wait.

Jake was right, Jane couldn't get him out of her head. She was worried about how Jake had acted at the party and felt like she needed to do something to help her soon-to-be former husband. Their divorce was still ongoing. On the Thursday that followed after the engagement party, Jane knew she needed to visit Jake. She wanted Reece's blessing first though. So that evening, she sat him down and told him.

"Absolutely not." Reece firmly gave Jane her answer.

"He needs our help," Jane said, shocked by Reece's lack of empathy for Jake, "You of all people should understand what he's going through."

"What's that supposed to mean?" Reece replied, leaning back in his seat, and crossing his arms.

"The drinking Reece," She said, "You could see from a mile off that he'd been drinking."

"No," He said back, standing up from his seat,

"You're not going."

"You can't control what I can and can't do Reece," She told him, standing up as well, "If I want to see him then I will."

Reece recognised that tone from when they had first slept together. This was the side of Jane that he didn't like. Her powerful and authoritative side. She slipped into it every time that she felt like she was losing control of a situation. Reece shook his head at her and walked away. Jane sat back down.

She didn't want to go against his wishes, but for Jake's sake, she had to.

That evening they went to bed and barely spoke. Jane slept with her back facing Reece. She was disgusted by his response to her wanting to see and help Jake. It was the two of them sleeping together that caused this to happen to Jake. Whilst she loved Reece and their unborn baby, she couldn't help but think what life would have been like for her if she hadn't told Jake to tutor Reece all those months ago. Then again though, 'everything happens for a reason, right?'

Friday 10th November 2017.

Jane awoke late the next morning. She wasn't at work, so she was able to get a lie-in. Reece had already gone out. He usually woke her up to say goodbye before he left for work, but he never bothered. Jane lay there for a while, trying to think of what to do. She cared about Jake and would hate herself if anything happened to him. Still, she loved Reece and didn't want to risk their relationship over a visit to Jake. Even though it was her fault that Jake was in the state that he was in.

Jane headed downstairs to the kitchen to make herself a drink. She saw a coin on the side and knew how she could solve her dilemma. A simple case of heads or tails. If it landed on heads, she would go to visit Jake. If it was tails, she wouldn't see him. So, she balled her hand into a fist and put her thumb just under her index finger. She rested the coin on there. She flicked upwards, launching the coin into the air. She caught it and laid it onto her forearm, keeping her hand over the top. Slowly, she moved her hand away.

Tails.

"Best of three." Jane said to herself, dissatisfied with the result. She picked the coin up and flipped it once more.

Tails again.

She put the coin on the worktop of the kitchen and carried on drinking her drink. She wasn't happy with the outcome but that's what fate had decided for her. She sat back in the living room and for the next half an hour she did nothing but mull over the decision in her head. In the end, she knew what she needed to do.

Jane went upstairs, got changed, and then she came back down and grabbed her car keys out of the dish by the front door. Jane went out of the house, knowing that Reece wouldn't be back until the evening, and drove to Jake's.

She reversed onto the drive and parked in front of the gate. The house was in darkness. Jane approached the front door and knocked it three times. She got an eerie, cold chill, travel down her spine. A feeling that she wasn't supposed to be there came over her. Reece had told her not to go. Fate had told her not to go. Jane paused for a moment and then turned around. Suddenly, she stopped. Jane heard the sound of the front door unlock. As she turned around, the door opened.

"Jane," Jake said, slurring his words slightly, "Come in."

Jane smiled and walked into her old home with her head down. Jake shut the door behind her.

"Can I get you anything to drink?" Jake asked, walking past her and into the kitchen.

"Just some water please." Jane replied. She looked Jake up and down and was completely stunned. Scruffy clothes, untrimmed beard. Jake looked like he had been dragged through a bush. Jake filled up a glass with water from the tap and put it on the side next to her. Jane put her car keys next to the glass.

"What are you doing here?" Jake asked her, scratching his beard.

"I just wanted to check on you," Jane told him, "I was worried about you."

"Why?" Jake smiled at her, grabbing a bottle of beer out of the fridge, and moving over to the drawer where the bottle opener was. Jane walked over and snatched the bottle out of his hand.

"This is why," She snapped, "You stunk of this stuff at the party."

Jake looked down at the floor, ashamed, "I'm sorry."

Jane put the bottle in the bin.

"You need to get a hold of yourself Jake," She said, "You're spiralling."

"I'm fine," He said, reaching into the bin and grabbing the bottle, "You're stressing as always."

Jane was dumbfounded by Jake getting the bottle out of the bin. He rinsed it off under the tap.

"I'm in complete control of this, Jane." Jake told her.

"No, you're not." She replied.

"Why are you so worried all of a sudden?" Jake asked, "You and Reece put me in this situation after all."

Jane froze.

"Is that why you're doing this?" Jane said, "Because of me and Reece?"

Jake stared at her for a moment before speaking, choosing his next words.

"Well, I thought you were perfectly happy," He told her, opening the bottle, "It killed me. You two, so happy together, after what you'd done to me. But then, at the party, I saw how you looked at me. You still care about me."

Jane stood quietly. She couldn't tell Jake he was wrong. Jake took a step closer to her. His words were no longer slurred and instead of alcohol, he smelt of aftershave.

"You still love me, Jane." Jake said, putting his hand softly on her face and kissing her. Jane kissed him back. It was true, she did love him. Suddenly, she pushed him back.

"What are you doing?" She shouted, "I'm with Reece."

"Then why didn't you stop me sooner?" Jake asked her. Jane couldn't give him an answer.

Jake then reached into his pocket and pulled his phone out. He unlocked the screen in front of Jane. She couldn't believe her eyes. Jake had been recording the entire conversation.

Jake pressed the red, square, button on his screen to end the recording.

"What is that?" Jane asked, trembling.

"Oh, it's nothing," Jake told her, "I'm sure Reece won't believe me anyway."

Jane started to panic. "Delete that Jake, now."

Jake shook his head.

"I bet he doesn't know you're here," Jake said, "Does he?"

"Delete it. Now." She told him, sternly.

Jake smiled at her and went to share the video with Reece.

"If you do this Jake," Jane said, "You'll regret it."

"Oh, will I Jane?" Jake replied, "How so?"

"You will." She told him. Jane started to slip back into that persona she invented all those months ago.

She could sense herself losing control of the situation. Reece couldn't get that recording. It could be the end of them. The end of their relationship. At this point, for Jane, rational thinking was out of the window.

"Oh, I'm so scared Jane," Jake teased, "The woman who couldn't even kill a spider is threatening me."

Jane wasn't used to this. Jake was immune to her persona. Her threats scared Reece, and she gave him a reason to believe she would do as she said. She just needed to give Jake a reason.

"I mean it Jake," She said, "You do this, and I will make you wish you hadn't."

Jake stopped and stared at her. This wasn't the Jane he knew. She was different. Jake smiled and continued to goad her into a reaction.

"I'm not scared of you Jane," He stated, "There's nothing you could say or do to scare me. I know you too well."

"Obviously not well enough," Jane declared, "You remember Ryan?"

"Reece's friend?" He answered, slightly puzzled at the angle she was taking, "What about him?"

"It was me." Jane told Jake who chuckled nervously, hitting record on his phone.

"What are you on about?" Jake replied, stepping back from her.

"He's dead because of me," She responded, "I killed him."

14 RYAN

Thursday 29th June 2017.

It was four days after Reece and Jane had slept together. Jane thought she had gotten it through to Reece that he was not to tell Jake about their little 'incident.' Reece had been trying his best to avoid Jake, but the fact was he was a liability. Even after Jane's threats to him, he still had thoughts about telling Jake.

Only two days after their night together, Reece had texted Jane trying to tell her that they needed to tell Jake. He was not comfortable keeping their secret from him. Clearly, the threats hadn't gotten through. Jane needed to take precautionary measures in case Reece decided to spill the beans about their little secret. If it got out, her life would be ruined. Jake was forgiving, but cheating was the ultimate betrayal.

On the Thursday morning after they had slept together, Reece called Jane.

"Jane," Reece said as Jane answered the phone call, "I'm not going to be able to keep this secret any longer."

"You have to," Jane replied, "Or are you having doubts about my threats."

"You can't control me, Jane," Reece stated, "You can't scare me."

"Try me." Jane responded, ending the call. She needed to do something urgently before Reece told Jake. Clearly, her fear factor had started wearing off. She needed to take control back. Reece couldn't tell Jake. Jane's marriage would fall apart. Fear started washing over her.

"Get a hold of yourself Jane," She told herself, "Think."

Jane did her best thinking when she was out getting a drink. So that's what she did. She had all the free time in the world. After all, she was stopping in a hotel using money she'd been putting away in secret for a gift she planned on buying Jake.

He'd been wanting a new watch for the best part of two years. Every week he was putting money into savings. However, whenever he got to a reasonable amount, something would go wrong, and they would have to spend the money to fix things either around the house or on one of the cars. So, Jane started taking money out of their account and told Jake it was for shopping. She then hid the money and saved it up. That way, the temptation or need to use it would never be there for him.

Jane packed her handbag and put a spare change of clothes into her bag. The weather had said it was going to rain, and she had forgotten her waterproof coat. Plus, her only umbrella was still at their old house. At least, by taking some clothes with her, she would have something to change into if she got too wet.

Once she had gotten everything ready, Jane decided to catch the bus into town and stop for a drink at the local café.

Jane went to the counter and ordered a tea and went and sat over at a table near to the door. Jane's tea was bought over to the table she was sitting at. She sat, deep in thought, pondering what way she could make Reece believe she was serious. The fact was, she'd got no way of proving that she would do whatever she needed to do to save her marriage. She had never been faced with a situation like the one that she was in.

Jane sat in the café for an hour. She scrolled through her phone after finishing her panini which she had bought. She still couldn't think of what to do, so she started to get ready to leave.

Then, opportunity walked through the door. Ryan entered the café and headed straight for the counter. The thought that followed was pure evil.

Jane thought that if she could really hurt Ryan, or even just scare the life out of him, then that would be enough to make Reece believe her.

"No, I can't do that." Jane whispered to herself in complete disbelief that she could even think of something like that. That wasn't who she was.

Jane looked at her wedding ring and then back at her phone which was displaying her text conversation between her and Reece. Jane looked back up at Ryan, who was now collecting his drink from the counter. 'He was the one who had the fight with Jake which led to him going to prison. He was the trigger which started each of the events which led to her sleeping with Reece.' Jane desperately tried to justify to herself what she was about to do.

"Fuck it," She said to herself, "Whatever it takes."

Ryan was just leaving the café when Jane got his attention, waving at him.

"Jane," He said, "Never expected to see you here, how are you?"

"I could be better," She replied, "How about you?"

"Yeah, about the same." He answered, his tone indicating that he wasn't okay. Jane saw her scope of opportunity get wider. She invited him to sit down, which he did. The two of them started talking about their issues. It turned out, Ryan was having problems at work.

Just before he got to the café, Ryan had been in an argument with his boss over some outstanding cheques which he had been trying to chase up. No matter how hard he worked, it never seemed good enough. So, when his boss had degraded him in front of the whole office, Ryan snapped. Emotions flared and it ended with Ryan storming out and heading to the café to calm down for a while. He didn't plan on going back in for the rest of the day. Or at all for that matter. He felt totally degraded.

The two carried on talking for a while about different things. Jane was quite curious to find out about the incident which resulted in Jake going to prison. Ryan started to reveal everything, talking at her, and explaining what happened. Jane used this as her time to plan her next move. She needed to be calculated. When she had her plan thought out, she pretended to check the time on her watch.

"Shit, I'm going to be late!" Jane exclaimed as she started swiping through her phone. Jane was very good at thinking on her feet when she needed to.

"Late for what?" Ryan asked her, trying to calm her down.

"I'm supposed to be meeting my friends by the old windmill for an afternoon walk," She told him, "I'll never make it in time."

"Relax," Ryan said, picking up his coffee, "I'll drive you there, no problem."

"You'd really do that for me?" She asked.

"Of course." Ryan reassured her that everything would be okay.

"Thank you so much, you're a lifesaver!" Jane

reacted, hugging him as she got up.

They both took a short, five minute, walk back to the car park together. They got to Ryan's car which was an old Seat Leon. He opened the door and picked up some clothes off his front passenger seat where Jane was going to sit. Ryan threw the clothes into the back of the car.

"Excuse the mess," He told Jane, "You can put your handbag in the boot if you want."

"Thank you." Jane replied. She walked around the car to the boot which she opened up. The boot was empty, except for a couple of loose carrier bags. Jane placed her bag inside. She saw Ryan get into the car and checked around to see if anyone was looking.

Jane then reached into her purse and pulled out a pocketknife. One that she always carried with her for protection ever since she got robbed a few years ago. It was a traumatic experience for her, so, she carried the knife in the hope that she could avoid a repeat incident in the future. She put the knife into her waistband and covered it up using her clothes so that Ryan wouldn't spot it. Jane closed her bag and shut the boot.

Once Jane was buckled in, Ryan started the car and drove out of town. He headed towards the forestry where the old windmill was. The closer they got; the more Jane panicked deep inside. She needed to be in control, so she snapped herself into her powerful mindset. Jane regained focus and noticed that they were almost there.

"Just pull up in this lay-by." Jane said, pointing to where she wanted Ryan to stop. Ryan indicated and parked up. He put his handbrake on. Jane's heart started racing.

"Let me get some money for you." She said, acting like she was reaching into her pocket.

"No worries, Jane," Ryan said, "You don't need to pay me."

Jane pulled the knife out of her waistband, hands shaking as if she was in the Arctic. Ryan threw his hands straight up. The look on his face was pure fear.

Ryan was in shock. He was scared for his life. He'd never had a knife pulled out on him before and the closest he'd came to getting hurt was when Jake hit him with that bar all those years ago.

"Jane," Ryan took a deep breath and tried his best to remain calm, "What are you doing with that?"

"I'm sorry," She said, tears forming in her eyes, hands still shaking, "I made a mistake. I need to show them I can do whatever it takes."

Ryan could see that this wasn't her. He didn't know what her motive or reasoning was, but he knew that she didn't want to hurt him. So, he was patient. After all, his life was on the line. One wrong move, one wrong word, could be the difference between life and death.

"Listen to me Jane," He made sure his voice was nice and soothing, even though he felt like his heart was about to rocket out of his chest, "You don't have to do this. I won't tell anyone, I promise."

That right there was an issue for Jane, she needed him to tell Reece. If he wasn't going to tell anyone, what was the point in her doing all of this?

"I'm sorry." Jane said as more and more tears fell down her face. Ryan saw how upset she was. He slowly placed his palm out on top of the hand she was holding the knife in. He tried to lower the blade. Everything he was saying was a blur. Jane was focused on the knife and that was it. Suddenly, Jane snapped. She was losing control and needed to get it back. Jane thrust the knife forward, trying to get Ryan to flinch. Instead, she ended up pushing the knife further forward than she thought.

Ryan let out a scream of pain and opened the door of his car. Whilst she had been focusing on the knife, she completely missed that he had been taking off his seatbelt and planning his escape. Ryan fell out of the car and onto the dirt floor. Jane looked down at the knife and her hand and saw that they were covered in Ryan's blood. Jane took a second to compose herself and then got out of the car.

Ryan tried to run away in a bid to get help, however, he was hindered by the wound Jane had inflicted. He headed towards the footpath, hoping to lose her in the forest. Jane knew that hardly any cars, or people, came down this area at this time of day.

Ryan was bleeding heavily. Adrenaline could only get him so far. The more he tried to get away, the more he struggled. Ryan continued to look behind to see Jane closing in. She approached him slowly and, without thinking, slashed him in the back with the knife. Ryan would drop to the floor with a thud, letting out a second scream of pain. With his face in the dirt, he could feel himself losing more and more blood. Jane towered over him as he rolled over, clenching onto his side, trying to apply pressure to the wound. The blood was flowing through the gaps between his fingers.

At this point, Jane knew now that Reece would be terrified by what she had done to Ryan. However, the slow realization started to kick in about what she had done. She now needed to stop Ryan from telling anyone. After all, she could convince Reece easily about what she had done. All she needed to do was take a picture to show to Reece.

"Not a word," Jane said, holding the knife in her right hand and pointing it at him, "Don't think I won't finish this."

Jane needed Ryan to agree not say anything. Ryan was a calculated person though. He knew at this point, with the rate at that he was bleeding, he wouldn't be making it out of this alive either way.

"Rot in hell you psycho bitch." Ryan snapped at her. Jane couldn't believe what she'd just heard. She only planned on scaring Ryan. She never wanted to kill him.

"Just agree Ryan," She pleaded with him, starting to Panic. Deep down, Jane had a gut feeling about what was coming, "Just agree not to say anything."

Ryan removed his hand from his side so that Jane

could see the extent he was bleeding. When she stabbed him, she pushed the knife in further than she planned to. She had lost her focus, and this was how she was paying for it.

"Make it quick." Ryan told her. Jane was reluctant. She looked down at the knife and back at Ryan. Seeing how much pain she had put him through, Jane felt as if she had no other choice.

Jane knelt down and pushed forwards with the knife, propelling it into Ryan's stomach. She looked into his eyes, watching on as the life drained out of them.

Jane froze for a moment and then threw herself back, dropping the knife by her side. She frantically tried to shimmy away from Ryan's lifeless corpse. She moved back until she was stopped by a tree. Jane looked on for a moment, wanting Ryan to get up and be okay. After about thirty seconds, Jane looked down at her hands and clothes, which were bloodied from her stabbing Ryan.

"No," She said, crying, "No, no, NO!"

Jane sat panicking for a moment and then realised that she needed to cover it up. Jane got to her feet and ran to Ryan's car. She opened the boot and looking around for anything that could help her. She opened up one of the carrier bags and found some gloves. Perfect.

Jane put the gloves on and ran back over to the body and started to drag him out to the woods. She needed somewhere that he wouldn't be found.

Burning him would risk a forest fire. She couldn't bury him as she didn't have a shovel. So, she dragged his body out to the forest and then ran away, not looking back. On her way back to the car, she picked up the blood-soaked knife that she had used to murder him.

She then got into Ryan's car and drove it five miles away from where she had left his body. She then parked up and waited for a while to see if any cars would come past. Nobody did. She had spotted some wipes in his car which she used to clean as much of the blood off of her as she possibly could. Jane then grabbed her handbag and routed through the clothes she had with her. Jane stopped, realising she would easily get recognised in them.

Jane tried to think. Ryan had thrown some clothes into the back of the car. She ran around to the front of the car and reached through from the driver's side, grabbing them. A blue tee shirt, black jacket, and some black elasticated tracksuit bottoms. Jane ran out into the forest and changed her clothes. She put her clothes into a ball and threw them into the back of his car. She carried on rooting through the car and found a lighter. She had an idea. She was surrounded by trees and branches, and her clothes were flammable too. Jane went and grabbed a branch, testing to see how easy it would catch fire. Unlike the weather had predicted, it hadn't rained yet, which meant that all twigs and branches on the floor were dry. She held the lighter to the branch. However, it didn't maintain the fire long enough for it to be effective.

Jane had another thought. She ran back to the car and grabbed the tee shirt which she had taken off earlier. She wrapped it around a stick that she found on the floor.

Jane ran back over to the car and opened the fuel cap, realising that petrol could help to ignite and maintain the fire that she needed. She took the top out, which barely had any petrol on, and set it alight using the lighter. Then, there was fire.

Jane grabbed her handbag out of the car and headed to the driver's side of the car. She then threw the now flaming branch and tee shirt through onto her pile of clothes which instantly caught fire. Jane ran away into the woods where she could watch the car burn from a distance where she wouldn't be seen. The car burnt out within twenty minutes.

Shortly after, Jane followed a path to the nearest village. On the way, she threw the knife that she had used to kill Ryan. She threw it so far into the forest that there would be no hope of it being recovered any time soon. From there, she caught a bus back to her hometown.

Jane got off the bus and walked straight to Reece's and banged on the door. Reece opened the door and she let herself in.

"Jane," He said, "What are you doing here?"

Jane turned around and looked at him, eyes red. Reece looked her up and down and then instantly noticed something.

"Is that," He stuttered, "Is that Ryan's top?"

Jane didn't say anything, she just stared.

"Who's blood is that?" He asked pointing at the top. Jane stood in silence. Reece started to piece together and ran straight for the phone. Jane intercepted him, pushing him to the floor.

"Have you told Jake?" She asked frantically as if she was possessed, Reece looked up at her in horror, "HAVE YOU TOLD JAKE?"

"NO," He shouted back, "What have you done Jane?"

"I told you that you shouldn't tell him," She said, "I FUCKING TOLD YOU."

Jane dropped to the floor and burst into tears instantly. Reece started crying, realising what she had done.

"I didn't mean to," Jane sobbed uncontrollably, "It was an accident, Reece, honestly."

"What the fuck, Jane?" Reece snapped back at her. Then, he could see Jane was genuinely distraught. He wanted to be angry at her. He wanted to report her. His feelings for her got the better of him. Jane continued sobbing.

"I just wanted to scare him," She said, "I needed you to know you couldn't tell Jake."

It was crazy what she had done. Reece couldn't quite believe it. In fact, it was more of a case that he didn't want to.

"Jane," He said, slowly approaching her and trying to see if she had anything on her which could hurt him, "Go upstairs and take a shower."

Jane looked up and glared at him, "No, you'll call the Police."

Jane shot to her feet and looked for the landline. She grabbed it off the side and pulled the battery out, throwing both the battery and the phone across the room.

"Jane, calm down," He said, "I'm not going to say anything. Just take a shower."

Jane stretched her hand out. "Phone. Now."

Reece got his phone out of his pocket and gave it to Jane. She went up the stairs and got into the shower. She was in there for over an hour, sobbing her heart out. When she got out, Reece had left her some of his clothes at the door. She got into them and went downstairs, holding Ryan's clothes in her hands.

Reece had turned on the log burner outside and asked for the clothes. She held them tight, refusing to let go. Reece showed Jane to the log burner, and she threw Ryan's clothes in there. After leaving them to burn, they both went and sat in the living room.

"Why are you helping me?" Jane asked Reece, who still had tears in his eyes.

"I don't know," He said, "I could tell you'd made a mistake, I've made tons in the past. Poor decisions for the right reasons. So, I could see on your face that, even though what you've done is wrong, you had a good reason at heart."

Jane sat quietly.

"But why Jane?" He asked, "Why go after Ryan?"

"He was in the café that I was in when I was trying to think of how to make you believe me." She explained, "I didn't want you to tell Jake. But it was a complete coincidence that he was there."

"Where is he now?" Reece asked. Jane glared over and Reece held his hands up, "You don't have to tell me, but he was my friend."

Jane sighed, "By the old windmill. He won't be found for a while."

The two sat in silence. Reece couldn't believe he'd helped her. Deep down though, he was blinded by love, just like she was. They somehow understood each other. In their own twisted way, they did everything out of love.

Reece had already lost the love of his life once when his wife left due to his drinking problems. He wasn't going to lose someone else that he loved.

The two sat in the house for a while after and were speechless. The house was in silence. Jane stayed for another thirty minutes and then left, heading back to the hotel she was staying at.

One thing was for sure. Reece definitely wouldn't be telling Jake anything now he knew what Jane was capable of.

15 JANE

Friday 10th November 2017.

Jane finished explaining how she killed Ryan. Jake stood in the kitchen, frozen to the spot. He couldn't believe what he was hearing.

"Bullshit," Jake replied, "That's not even funny."

"It's true," She told Jake, "Go ahead. Send that to Reece. It'll be the last thing you ever do."

Jake could see in Jane's eyes that she was telling the truth. Evil occupied a space where he once saw love. Jane was a cold-blooded killer. Jake stood in silence for a moment. Jane felt content. She had finally regained control over him.

"All that," Jake said to Jane, "Just to cover up your dirty one-night stand?"

Jane was stunned at his outburst.

"That one-night stand was your fault!" She

countered, trying to shift the blame on to Jake, "If you hadn't have stormed out then none of this would have ever happened."

"Don't you dare go pinning this on me," He screamed back at her, "You're the psycho who murdered Ryan!"

"Psycho?" She answered. It bought back the memories of when she killed Ryan all those months ago, "How dare you."

"Why?" Jake asked, "It's clearly fucking true."

Jane froze. She couldn't frighten Jake one bit. Even after this revelation.

"You're a fucking psycho bitch!" He shouted back at her. He barged past her, heading to the landline.

"Where do you think you're going?" Jane shouted, "I'm not done with you yet."

Jake turned around, "No, but I'm done with you."

Jake spun back around and headed for the living room. Jane looked over at the side and saw the glass which Jake had given her earlier. In a state of panic, Jane grabbed the glass and headed straight towards Jake. She smashed the glass over the back of his head. With that, Jake dropped to the floor.

Jane looked down for a moment and saw Jake wasn't moving. She dropped straight down to her knees and shook him.

"Jake?" Jane said, trying to get his attention, "Wake up."

Jane tried shaking him again, but he was unresponsive. She put her hand around the back of his head to feel it was wet. Jane moved her hand from his head and looked down at it. Blood.

Jane started panicking. She'd done it again. Just like Ryan, she had killed Jake. Jane rushed to get a brush from up the corner of the kitchen.

She swept up the glass and threw it into the bin. She looked back at Jake, who was still lay on the floor. Anxiety washed over her. Jane ran to the front door and left the house, heading straight for her car. She tried frantically to open the door, but it wouldn't open.

"Shit!" She exclaimed to herself, realising she had forgotten to pick up her keys. Jane bolted back into the house, leaving a bloody hand mark on the door handle of her car.

Jane grabbed her keys off the side and took another look to where she left Jake. However, he wasn't there. Jane looked around frantically. Jake could be anywhere. She went into the drawer and grabbed a knife, holding it tightly in her hand in case Jake popped out. Jane's heart started pounding out of her chest. She rounded the doorframe into the living room, only to see that Jake wasn't in there. Jane slowly headed out of the house, remaining on full alert for him. Nothing. Jake wasn't in sight.

Jane got to the front door and ran out to her car, clicking the unlock button several times as fast as she could. She jumped into her car and started the engine, locking the doors and putting her seatbelt on as she pulled away. Jane threw the knife onto the passenger seat next to her. 'Where could he have gone? Who is he going to tell?'

Jane carried on driving, foot to the floor. It was getting dark now. She took a sharp right turn down some country lanes, causing any loose items to fall.

Jane had to try and think of what to do next. Jake was somewhere out there and was fully aware of what she had done. Jane turned onto a dark, unlit, road. The road was meant to be big enough for two cars, but she drove it as if it were a one-way street.

"FUCK!" Jane shrieked, realising the gravity of the situation she was in. She approached a sharp bend in the road when suddenly, she felt a sharp pain cut across her throat. Jane put her hand to her neck and felt it was wet. She pulled her hand away and looked down. Blood.

She looked back up and saw she was approaching a telegraph pole in excess of forty miles per hour. With no time to brake, she tried to avoid it and lost control of the car, causing it to skid and hit the pole side on. Jane's airbag went off on impact. She lifted her head out of the blood-stained airbag to see her rear driver's side door slowly start to open.

A shadowy figure emerged from out of the back. It was Jake. He had been hidden in the footwell behind her seat. Jane hadn't even noticed that Jake was in the car. She was in that much of a rush to get away. Only now, it was too late.

Jane looked over to her left for the knife, but it was nowhere to be seen. She tried to scream for help but couldn't because of the cut to her throat. She was powerless. Defenceless. Jake opened the driver's side door of her car. She looked at him, teary-eyed.

"You did this," He said, "You and your state of always having to be in control."

Jane sat there, unable to speak, holding onto her throat and applying pressure to the cut. She was trying to slow the bleeding. Trying to delay the inevitable. Every second that passed by her felt like a minute.

"You ruined my life!" Jake yelled at her, passion burning in his voice, "I never wanted this!"

Jake looked down at the bloodied knife. He'd managed to avoid the spray of blood, as it sprayed over the steering wheel and the windscreen.

"I loved you Jane," He said with anguish, "I loved you so fucking much. You betrayed me. You and Reece."

Silence filled the air around them for a moment. All that could be heard was the sound of Jane's car, trying to keep itself alive after the heavy impact, much like Jane.

"All this time I've been trying to get revenge on Reece," Jake told her, "But now I realise. You're as much to blame as he is."

Jane put her hands together, trying to make a praying motion towards Jake. She tried to plead with him without using the words she couldn't speak. Her life was in his hands. He could still do the right thing. Jake looked into her eyes, trying desperately to find one last sign that she loved him. He just saw fear. He saw that she realised this was the end.

Tears continued to flow from Jane's eyes as Jake stared into them. Jake made his mind up. He slammed the driver's door shut and walked away from her and around the car. Jane stomped desperately on the floor of the car, trying to get his attention. Jake ignored her. He opened the boot and found a thin towel in there. He took it out and cut it in half with the knife he had used to slit Jane's throat. Jake then rolled it up and shut the boot.

Jane watched in her mirror as Jake opened up the fuel cap of her car and stuffed the freshly-cut towel down it. Panic engulfed her as she saw him pull the lighter out. Jake took one last look in the car's wing mirror, making contact with Jane's eyes for one last time.

Memories flickered through his mind like a photo album. The time they first met, all the dates they shared, movie nights, and their big wedding day. The came the memories of Jane betraying him. Their weekend away when he found out she had slept with Reece. Years of love. Years of compassion. Gone.

A single tear made its way down Jake's cheek. He mouthed the words 'I love you' to her one last time, and then set fire to the towel. Jake ran away into the countryside.

Desperation filled Jane as she kicked and stomped and tried to get out of the car. Jake had completely forgotten, but Jane was fighting for two people. Jane managed to get the driver's door open. She tried to get out, but it was too late. The car burst out into flames, consuming Jane in the process. Jake watched from afar, tears welling up in his eyes. The love of his life. Gone.

Jake turned around and made his way home. He stopped off at a local payphone and called the Police, informing them that there had been some sort of crash. He gave details of the location and that was it. He hung the phone up, without providing any of his details.

Police, Ambulance, and the Fire service didn't take long to get to the scene. They cordoned off the road and got investigators out to look at the crash. They couldn't tell that Jane's throat had been slit because of the fire. At the same time though, they couldn't quite figure out how the car had caught fire.

Her body was taken to the coroner to be checked and the car was hauled away to a Police forensic facility. They were able to identify who she was at the scene of the incident based on the identification number on the car. Somehow, it was one of the only things to have survived the fiery explosion. Police identified a next of kin. Reece.

Police arrived at Reece's house in the early hours of the morning. They knocked on Reece's door. Three solid knocks that Reece would never forget. Three knocks that would haunt him for the rest of his life.

Reece opened the door to see two uniformed

officers on the other side. Both would simultaneously take their hats off. Reece instantly knew why they were at his house. Jane hadn't been home all day and wasn't answering his texts or his calls.

Reece collapsed to the ground, breaking out into tears. His world shattered into tiny pieces. After everything that Reece did to try and get back on his feet. He finally managed to get through all the loss he had suffered. He finally started to have everything he ever wanted. In the matter of a few moments, everything was gone. Once again, Reece was completely alone.

16 CONDOLENCES

Friday 10th November 2017.
Jake
'What have I done?' Jake asked himself over and over again. He knew he had gone too far. He could quite easily have stopped himself. Jane might have been ready to kill him, but he wasn't ready to kill Jane.

He opened a bottle of beer and started to drink, waiting for the nightmare to end. Eventually, he realised that this was his reality. That this nightmare was his life. He'd lost all control of his emotions and had finally snapped. For his whole life, Jake had controlled himself as best as he possibly could. Sure, he lost it a couple of times, but he always recovered. Not this time. Jake knew it. He was broken.

That night he never slept. Instead, he sat waiting for the Police to arrive. Even though there were no camera's around when he killed Jane, he thought it was only a matter of time until the Police found out what really happened and came after him. Jake knew one thing though now. Jane's death couldn't be in vain. Despite the plan drifting wildly off course, he needed to stick with it. Now wasn't just about hurting Reece to win Jane back. Now, it was about revenge.

Saturday 11th November 2017.
Reece

Reece was helped up off the floor by the officers. Tears blurred his vision. Loss clouded his judgement. Reece went straight into the living room, unlocked the cupboard, and grabbed the bottle of Whiskey that Jake had bought him. The officers stopped him.

"Don't do it kid." The officer told him, putting his hand on his shoulder as Reece held the bottle by the neck. The officer slowly reached over and grabbed the bottle.

Reece held onto it initially but let it go after a few seconds. The officer put the bottle back in the cupboard and locked it back up. He could instantly tell from thirty-plus years of experience that Reece had issues with alcohol. The one officer guided him down to a seat and the other officer went and put the kettle on to make a drink. The officer handed Reece a tissue.

"How did it happen?" Reece asked, blowing his nose with the tissue, and using his sleeve to wipe his eyes.

"It was a car accident," The officer told Reece, "We suspect that she lost control on a country lane, swerved and hit a telegraph pole."

Reece carried on shedding tears. The officer didn't want to say the next part, but Reece needed to know.

"The car burst into flames, Jane seemed to have made it out but it was too late." The officer said, putting his head down. Reece gasped for air, unable to comprehend what he had just heard.

"She," He said with shortened breaths as if he were breathing through a paper bag, "She burnt to death?"

The officer just put his head down, not wanting to give Reece the answer but implying that she did.

"I'm sorry." The officer told Reece, putting his hand on his shoulder and comforting him. Reece sobbed continually. The officers stayed with him as long as they could. They made him a couple of cups of tea.

The officers got up and held their hats in their hands, "Our condolences, Reece." The officers showed themselves out as Reece sat on the sofa. After the officers left, Reece stayed up most of the night. He couldn't sleep for ages because he couldn't stop crying. He did drop off to sleep eventually, only to be awoken by his normal ten o'clock morning alarm. The nightmare continued.

Reece struggled to get to grips with the news. He sat looking through his phone at pictures of him and Jane. Of memories which they had crafted together. It took him all of his strength not to turn to the bottle.

Jake

Jake paced around his kitchen, still drinking, unable to comprehend what he had done. He tried to sleep throughout the night, but every time he closed his eyes, he saw Jane's face begging for mercy. At midday, there was a knock on the door.

Jake started to panic. He wanted to check who was at his door, but he knew that, if it was the Police, they would see him at the windows. Jake waited, hoping whoever was knocking his door would leave. They didn't go. Instead, they knocked at the door again. This time, the knock was deeper.

Jake wiped his tears and headed to the door. He slowly opened the door and was somewhat relieved to see that Reece was on the other side.

"Reece," Jake fully extended the door, "What're you doing here?"

Reece just looked at the floor, "Am I okay to come in?"

"Of course." Jake let Reece in. Reece went straight into the living room without saying anything further and sat down. Reece's eyes were bright red and the look on his face was one of pure defeat. Instantly, Jake knew what this was about. Despite knowing what had happened, Jake dreaded to hear the news.

"I'll put the kettle on." Jake said, walking into the kitchen and filling the kettle up. He flicked the switch and heated up the water. Jake looked back over through the door and saw Reece with his head in his hands. Jake finished making the drinks and took them into the living room. He placed a cup of tea in front of where Reece was seated and sat down opposite him. Reece took a moment as he tried to find the words to say.

"Jane's dead." Reece said it bluntly, not being able to find any other way to tell Jake. Jake acted as if he was in shock.

"What?" Jake replied, pretending that this was news to him. His verbal response may have been fabricated, but his feelings were real, "How?"

Reece looked over at Jake, "She had a crash, and swerved into a telegraph pole." He didn't think that Jake needed to know that Jane had burnt to death. It was something that he wished that he had never found out himself.

"Oh my gosh," He acted like this was the first time he found out about the news.

"Yeah," Reece responded, "I can't believe it."

The two sat in silence for a moment. Reece was still digesting the news, Jake was still struggling,

"Are they sure it was Jane?" He asked, "Surely it would have been hard for them to recognise her."

Reece froze for a moment, "What do you mean? I never told you she burnt to death."

Jake realised he had slipped up. He needed to correct himself, and fast.

"I'll be honest with you," Jake said, sitting forwards, "The Police came round this morning and told me, I just didn't want to believe it."

Reece stared at Jake for a moment, and then sat back.

"That's sort of a weight off my shoulders," Reece replied, seeming relieved, "I've been wondering how to tell you all morning."

"I couldn't believe it," Jake told Reece, "I still can't."

The two sat in silence for a while after that. They mourned the loss of Jane. She was the love of both of their lives. Jake struggled with the guilt even more being face-to-face with Reece.

Reece was struggling to be at Jake's as he was surrounded by pictures of Jane and empty bottles of alcohol. Realising that he needed to leave, Reece finished his drink and the two shook hands, agreeing to put their differences behind them. Reece left and Jake ran straight upstairs and threw up in the toilet. He had been holding it in the whole time that Reece was there.

Over the course of the next week, Jake and Reece worked together for Jane's funeral. They met up every day. Reece wanted to support Jake, and Jake wanted to earn Reece's trust. Jake and Reece slowly became friends. Jake subconsciously blamed Reece for Jane's death, despite the fact that he was the one who murdered Jane. It was like the old times for them, meeting up and going to the pub. Reece didn't drink whilst he was there, but Jake did.

Monday 20th November 2017.

Jake suited up in all black, for today was the day of Jane's funeral. By this point, Jake was consumed by both pain and guilt. There was a big part of Jake which wanted him to get caught for what he had done.

He went to Reece's and parked his car on the drive. The hearse was to be attending with Jane's coffin in the back. For Reece, he was going to two funerals that day. Jane's funeral, and the funeral for their unborn child. Jake never thought of that though. He was trying not to. It just added to the guilt that he was feeling.

Jake knocked on Reece's door but there was no answer. Jake tried the door handle and it opened. He walked through the house to see Reece seated in the living room. He appeared to be having a staring contest with the bottle of Whiskey which Jake had bought for him as his engagement gift.

"It's not going to get finished that way," Jake told Reece who then snapped out of his trance and glared over at Jake, "Sorry, completely forgot."

"It's okay," Reece told Jake, putting the bottle of Whiskey into the cupboard and locking the door, "I do it as a measure."

Jake looked puzzled, "What do you mean?"

"Well," Reece started to explain, "It's a showing of how far I've come. Every time I'm faced with a challenge that I don't think I can overcome; I get the bottle out and just stare at it. Knowing that I don't open it, gives me strength."

"That's good Reece," Jake was impressed, he nodded at Reece, "She would be proud."

"I miss her so much." Reece replied, getting teary.

"Me too." The two of them shared a hug. Shortly after, the hearse arrived. Reece couldn't leave the house at first. He wished he had Jake's confidence with this sort of thing. Jake hugged Reece, trying to support him as much as possible. Reece grabbed a photograph off the side as he got to the front door. Jake opened the door and the two walked out to the hearse.

Reece broke out into tears at the sight of Jane's name which was beautifully arranged using white flowers and rested against the side of her coffin. Jake supported Reece, helping him to the back of the hearse where Reece rested the photograph up against the coffin. The photograph was one of him and Jane which they taken just after they got engaged. In it was one of the copies of their baby scan. Seeing the picture left a lump in Jake's throat. He felt like he needed to throw up. Instead, he had to hold it in. His guilt continued to burn like a raging fire in his gut.

Reece wiped his tears and stepped back from the coffin. He got into the car behind which was part of the cortege. They followed as part of the procession. They parked up at the entrance to the church where the doors were already open. Jake and Reece, along with a couple of Jane's other distant family members, carried her coffin into the church where the service began.

It was a tough moment for both Reece and Jake for different reasons. Reece was suffering from two catastrophic losses whilst Jake was suffering from an immeasurable amount of guilt as well as the pain of losing the love of his life.

Afterwards, they attended the wake at Fradley's arms. It was mainly Jane's family. Some of Jake's were there too, as were Reece's.

After the funeral, Jake and Reece headed back to Reece's house. Jake slept on the sofa downstairs. In the morning, when he made sure Reece was okay, he left. He got back home and looked at a photograph of Jane, stroking her cheek as if she were really there in front of him. He shed a tear, and then the memories all came flying back into his head. Not happy memories though. The memory of their last argument. The crash. The flames. All of it. Haunting him. 'How had it all come to this?' Jake thought to himself.

He looked for someone, or something, to blame for everything that had happened. Jake had tried as much as he could to shift his guilt, but he couldn't. He still blamed Reece for how everything went down.

Jake fell into a deep sleep on the next evening due to the lack of sleep from previous nights. During his sleep, Jake had a dream.

He was standing in his living room looking out of the window to see the sun shining. Jake turned around to notice Jane standing in the doorway holding a cup of tea, wearing the green dress and nametag from when they first met.

"Hi Jake," Jane said in her sweet and innocent voice. Jake was confused, unaware that he was dreaming. It felt so real to him.

"Jane," Jake replied, "You're alive?"

Jane didn't say anything. She just smiled. Jake ran over to Jane and gave her a hug, not wanting to let her go.

From where he was standing, Jake could just see a pool of blood in the kitchen. He started to become disillusioned, confused by what was going on. Just then, he felt a slow wave of heat fly over his back.

Jake turned around to the source of the heat to notice Reece standing there screaming.

"JANE!" Reece yelled out in desperation. Jake turned back around in shock to see he was no longer standing in the living room but on the road where he killed Jane. Jake looked on in horror as he saw Jane's car burning. Just then, he saw Jane crawl out of the driver's side of the car.

Jake rushed over to her, hoping to pull her from the wreckage of the car. Jake sat on the ground next to her and cradled Jane in his arms.

"How could you do this Jake?" Jane asked with her final breath as she died in his arms. Jake let out a scream on pain, having to watch Jane die for a second time. Jake stood back up to get pushed back down to the ground by a young Reece who was accompanied by Ryan, Fred, Olly, and Jason. As they all towered over him, Jake was transported back to his childhood. Jake jumped to his feet and started running.

As he ran, he passed a nearby car accident. He didn't have time to stop and look. He just saw two cars near to a round-a-bout.

The next thing Jake knew, he was inside the church where they held Jane's funeral. Jake was facing the altar, looking at the crucifix. Jake begged for forgiveness. Then, the doors creaked open, and a bright light made its way into the church.

Jake looked on as the light dimmed to reveal Reece standing there. Jake watched as Reece walked over to Jake with a smirk on his face. The same smirk he used to have when he bullied Jake in school. Jake felt himself welling up with rage. He went to punch Reece, only to fall down to the floor.

No matter where he was, he couldn't escape Reece.

Jake woke up panting. He looked around for a moment to make sure that he wasn't still trapped in the vivid nightmare. He headed downstairs to grab a glass of water from the tap.

Jake was unsure what to make of the dream. He felt guilty for what he had done. At the same time though, he still felt anger towards Reece.

He wasn't done with him yet. Jake still needed revenge. All he needed to do was to bait Reece out.

Thursday 23rd November 2017.

Jake hadn't seen, or heard, from Reece since the

funeral. He bought some flowers to take to his house. Jake parked up outside, got out and knocked on the door but there was no answer. He looked through the windows of the house, but there were no signs of life. Reece's car was on the drive, and he didn't really go to the pub anymore, so he had to be in.

Jake stood up against the door, using his back to lean up against it. The guilt had just kept building and building inside him, knowing that this was Jane's home too. Then, Jake knew how he could bait Reece out. He turned around and stood up against the door.

"I did it," Jake said quietly, "I killed Jane."

Whilst part of Jake said it to bait Reece out, there was a big part of him which also said it out of guilt. He figured if he said it out loud, then it would ease his suffering. Jake didn't know what else to say after that.

He left the flowers on the floor, turned around, and walked back to his car. Tears streamed from his eyes as he pulled away from the kerb and started to drive away.

The door opened and Reece watched Jake drive away. He had heard everything, just as Jake planned.

'How had Jake killed Jane?' Reece asked himself. He picked the flowers up off the floor and headed back into his house where he threw them across the kitchen in a fit of rage.

'What did he mean?'

Thoughts circled Reece's head like sharks. Reece tried to deny it, but after finding out that Jane had killed Ryan, anything could happen.

Reece thought and thought. Then it clicked. The day when he told Jake about Jane's death, he already knew that she had burnt to death. Reece tried to dig deeper. Jake's response wasn't as emotional as what Reece thought it would have been. Thoughts continued to fly in and out of his head.

'But Jake said the Police had been round to his house,' Reece thought, still trying to negate what he heard Jake say at the door.

Then, another thought popped into his head. 'He could have lied, he lied to Jane about prison for all those years.' Reece didn't know what to think.

He headed straight over to the drawer and grabbed the key for the cupboard. He opened it, snatching the bottle of Whiskey from out of the cupboard and slammed it onto the table. He grabbed a glass from the kitchen and placed that next to the bottle. He needed to resist. He needed to fight the urge. It was consuming him. The battle between the demons in his head was heavy on him. Almost like torment. He could feel an angel telling him not to drink, but the devil was telling him to drink.

Reece caved in. He unscrewed the cap and poured a glass. He waited for a moment. He had come so far. To beat his addiction. To resist the urge to drink. Reece had proved his strength to himself. However, he still felt weak. He looked over at a picture of Jane.

Then, he heard a voice, fighting through the voices of the demons in his head. It was Jane.

"Don't do it Reece." The voice in his head told him. Jane's voice told him. It felt so real, almost like she was sat next to him. Reece knew that it was all in his head, but those few words gave him the strength he needed.

Reece picked up the glass and the bottle and took them into the kitchen. He poured both of them down the sink and threw the bottle outside where it smashed into tiny pieces.

This time, Reece was at the wheel.

This time, Reece was in control.

Whatever he would do next was up to him.

17 WANTING THE TRUTH

Over the course of the next few days, Reece sat and pondered his suspicions. He was struggling to get over Jake's revelation. He didn't want to believe what he had heard. 'He's lying' was all Reece kept thinking to himself, mulling over the moment again and again.

At this point he would have got the Whiskey bottle out, just to make sure that he was strong enough to carry on. He didn't need to do that anymore. He knew his strength.

Sunday 26th November 2017.
Reece couldn't get what Jake had said off his mind. As a method of distraction, he decided to clean the house. Reece was sorting through the drawers around the house and reorganising them.

Whilst clearing through one of his drawers, he

came across a photograph of Jane which she had asked him to put away. He loved the photo. He'd taken it on one of their various trips away. She was standing by the sea on the beach, letting the waves brush against her feet. Looking at the photograph took Reece straight back to that day.

He sat on the edge of the bed and stared at the picture for twenty minutes, tears slowly emerging from his eyes and forming down his cheek. The only problem was, every time he tried to think about Jane, he could only think about what he heard Jake say at the front door.

Reece knew that he had to try and confirm any suspicions which he had. He had to be secretive about it though. He didn't want Jake to know he was onto him, so he had to be coy. After all, Reece wasn't meant to hear Jake's confession, or so he thought.

He decided to pay Jake a visit to gauge his behaviour following his revelation. So later that day, Reece went to Jake's house.

Reece parked up on the drive and stared at the house for a moment. He got an eerie chill shiver down his spine. Almost like a presence telling him not to go any further. That he should just turn around and head home. Reece didn't listen to it though.

Instead, he got out the car and headed straight to the door. It only took him two knocks for Jake to answer, who actually appeared to be sober for a change.

"Hi Reece," he said, "Come in."

Reece walked in, nodding at Jake as he walked past. Jake directed him to the kitchen where he made a cup of tea for them both. They had a bit of general 'chit-chat' before heading into the living room and taking a seat on Jake's sofa. There were a few beer bottles in sight but not anywhere near as many as what Reece expected.

"So, to what do I owe the pleasure?" Jake asked. Reece knew that this was his chance. Reece thought that, because of Jake's confession at the door, he was feeling guilty. He just needed to put on the right amount of pressure to get Jake to crack.

"It's about Jane." Reece replied, watching to see how Jake's facial expression changed. It didn't.

"Go ahead," he replied, "I'm all ears."

"I just miss her so much," Reece said with real tears welling up in his eyes, "I miss her smile. Her hair. Her eyes. Everything about her."

Reece looked up at Jake, who nodded in understanding.

"I know how you feel," Jake replied, "Sure, we had our differences, but it doesn't change how much I loved her. Cared for her."

'He's not cracking,' Reece thought to himself, 'Time to put on the pressure.'

"I can't get my head around it though," Reece responded, looking Jake in the eyes, "How she died, she must have suffered."

It was hurting Reece to talk about it, but he needed to see Jake's true reaction for himself. Jake looked down.

"I try not to think about it." Jake told him.

"I mean, it's not natural," Reece replied, "How does a car even go up in flames like that?"

"I'd like to give you an answer," Jake continued to look down at his feet, "I honestly have no clue."

Jake was getting upset, but he wasn't cracking. Reece decided to cut his losses and change the subject to something else. It obviously required some more thought on Reece's behalf. 'Maybe that wasn't what Jake said. Maybe he didn't say anything at all.'

Admitting defeat, Reece decided to go. He made up an excuse to leave early. He headed home and carried on with some more housework to try and keep his mind occupied.

When Reece left, Jake did begin to stress. Whilst his plan was on track, he'd taken a huge risk by confessing to killing Jane. Especially at the fact that he'd done it within earshot of Reece. He knew for sure now that Reece had heard him.

Jake just needed to be patient now and see what Reece would do with the information. His plan now hinged on Reece's actions. In the meantime, he had to prepare for the next stage of his plan.

Monday 27th November 2017

Reece started back at work on Monday. Wanting to get back into his old routine. He'd forgotten what work was like. Since he got the job, he felt like he had taken more time off to grieve than he had been in work. He settled straight back in, trying not to think about Jane or what he thought Jake had said. He did well throughout the day, however, it was the night time when he started to struggle. Throughout the night, it started to bug him again.

Reece felt like he was going insane mulling it over in his head. He was one-hundred-and-ten per cent sure that Jake had said he killed Jane but couldn't figure out why Jake would want to do such a thing. Reece couldn't think of anything else. There was only one solution. Confront Jake.

'But what if he admits it? What's the plan then?' Thoughts spun through Reece's head like a Waltzer at a fairground. Reece wanted to confront Jake but continuously changed his mind. He had already tried putting pressure on Jake but that didn't work. Reece sat and thought but he couldn't formulate a plan. He tried again to stop thinking about it but after a while but the it began to dominate his every thought. Reece couldn't think of anything else.

Deep down, he knew he needed to confront Jake. If Jake could kill Jane though, in the way that he did, Reece dreaded to think what he'd do to him. Reece went upstairs and pulled the ladder down into the loft. He climbed up. Waving his hand to clear the cobwebs, Reece looked around. He was on his hands and knees due to the room being too low for him to be able to stand up.

He looked around for a light switch. He knew that there was one up there, but he had no idea where it was. He headed back down the ladder and went to the kitchen in search of a torch which he managed to find in one of the drawers.

Reece headed back up into the loft where he started searching around, using the torch to light up the space. He moved box after box with no joy. Just as he was about to give up, Reece spotted the light switch. He flicked it on and lit the entire space up with a dim, yellow light. Then, he spotted it.

Reece pulled a wooden box out with a lock on it. He blew the dust off it to reveal an army-style pattern on the box from his time when he served. He located the key in another box nearby. Reece took the box down from the loft and placed it on his bed. He got dust everywhere, but he wasn't really bothered.

He unlocked the box to reveal a Glock seventeen semi-automatic pistol, already loaded with one magazine. It was black in colour. Reece had owned it for three years. It was the gun he used in the army, and after quitting he bought himself one to remind him of all the hard times he faced during his service. Losing friends, taking lives, and making sacrifices.

Now all that was needed was to meet with Jake. Reece picked up his phone and called him. A phone call that Jake had been sat waiting for. The final stage of Jake's masterplan was set to begin.

"Jake, it's Reece, can we meet?" Reece asked after hearing that Jake had answered.

"Sure," Jake replied, "My place in a few hours?"

Reece was on the back foot, but he didn't know.

FOLLOW IN MY FOOTSTEPS

Jake was one step ahead. Whilst his feelings kept changing, the plan never did. After Jane's death. After he had so brutally murdered her, Jake knew that he needed to follow this through. Otherwise, her death would have been for nothing.

"Sounds good," Reece told Jake, "See you shortly."

Jake ended the call and prepared for Reece's arrival.

Reece arrived at ten past seven in the evening. This time, he didn't pause on the drive. He was committed. He headed straight to Jake's door and knocked three times.

Jake opened the door and let him in. The two sat down and started talking. Reece had the pistol secreted in his waistband behind his back, covered by his tee shirt. Jake made them both drinks and the two took a sat down in the living room. They started talking and just had a general conversation for approximately twenty minutes.

The conversation was interrupted as Jake got up from where he was sat, grabbing his phone, he headed into the toilet. Reece looked around from where he was sat and spotted a box on the floor which was labelled 'Christmas.' The perfect conversation starter. Jake walked back into the room and sat down.

"Are you celebrating Christmas this year?" Reece asked, nodding towards the box.

"Yeah," Jake nodded, "Jane used to love it. I

couldn't let her down."

"I don't know how you can celebrate it," Reece replied, "Especially after everyone we've lost this year."

"I know," Jake replied, "It's been a massive shock."

Reece agreed, "I'm not celebrating, especially after losing Jane."

"And I bet losing the whole group has affected you too" Jake answered back.

'The whole group?' Reece thought to himself, "Well we've not lost everyone have we?"

Jake looked puzzled, "What do you mean?"

"Jason," Reece responded, watching Jake's facial expression change, "He's still alive."

"Ah yeah," Jake replied, "I'd forgot he was still kicking around."

Jake had tried to make a joke and brush it off but then, Reece thought to himself 'I haven't heard from Jason in a while, does Jake know something I don't?'

"What made you think Jason was dead?" Reece asked, more as if he were starting an interrogation against Jake.

"I don't," Jake said, his body language starting to change, as if he were more on edge. Little did he know, Jake was putting it on to lure Reece into a trap. He just needed Reece to get worked up and lash out, "It was just a mistake."

Reece noticed the change in Jake's body language, "Is there something you're not telling me?"

"Where's this coming from Reece?" Jake knew exactly where he was coming from, he had to make Reece feel that he had the upper hand though. Reece just stared at Jake, expecting him to know. There was a moment of silence, which was interrupted by the noise of Reece putting his drink down onto the table. Reece reached behind his back and pulled out the gun from his waistband.

Now, Jake wasn't expecting that.

Jake's hands instantly flew up into the air, "REECE, WHAT ARE YOU DOING?"

Reece aimed the gun at Jake's head, "Tell me the truth, Jake!"

"What truth?" Jake couldn't let his plan slip now, despite staring down the barrel of a Glock. He took deep breaths, trying to calm himself down.

"I know you killed Jane!" He shouted, standing up, gun still aimed at Jake's head, "But what's happened to Jason?"

"Killed Jane?" Jake asked, forcing tears out, "How dare you."

Jake said it with such conviction that it caused Reece to lower his guard for a split second. Jake saw that he had gotten through. Reece raised the gun back up.

"I heard you," Reece said, thrusting the gun forward slightly, "I heard you at my door say you killed Jane."

"I have no clue what you're on about Reece," Jake told him, "Are you okay?"

"Don't fucking ask me if I'm okay Jake," Reece snapped back, "I heard you say it at the door."

Jake stood up slowly, stretching his hand out. He could start to see the doubt in the back of Reece's mind.

"I didn't kill Jane," He said softly, placing his hand on the top of the gun, lowering it down and slowly releasing it from Reece's grip.

"I heard you," Reece cried out, "I know what I heard."

Jake had hold of the gun now, but he had no clue what to do with it. He placed it on the arm of the chair. Jake was wearing gloves, so his prints weren't on the gun. Once Reece had sat back down, Jake knew it was the perfect moment to strike.

"I'm going mad Jake," Reece said, "I'm losing it."

"No you're not," Jake said, as if he was reassuring Reece, "Trust me."

"How can you say that?" Reece replied through tears, "I just had a gun to your head!"

Jake sat back down and rested Reece's gun on the arm of the chair.

"Because you were right," He responded calmly. Now he had disarmed Reece, he could carry on with what he had planned, "You'd heard correctly."

Reece looked up in shock, unable to comprehend what he had just heard. He looked over at the gun. Jake noticed this and rested his hand on it. Then, Reece realized exactly what Jake had done. He'd waited until Reece was unarmed and then confirmed

Reece's suspicions. Reece started to catch on that Jake had planned this all along. Jake was the one in control. Not Reece.

"YOU FUCKER!" Reece yelled, jumping up and reaching for the gun. Jake stood up and grabbed the gun. He stepped to the side and aimed it at Reece.

"I'LL FUCKING KILL YOU," Reece shouted, feeling a variation of emotions flowing through him, "YOU BASTARD!"

"Relax, Reece," Jake continued to hold the gun towards Reece, "You came here wanting the truth did you not?"

Reece seethed, breathing like a bull ready to charge.

"Ask away," Jake replied calmly, "What were you asking about Jason earlier?"

Reece froze. 'Surely not.'

"You didn't," Reece told Jake, the hatred could be heard in his voice, "Don't you dare say it."

"I killed Jason too," Jake had a smugness to his voice, he was in control, and Reece's judgement was getting clouded by hate, "And you've had the murder weapon all this time."

Reece was confused. He thought hard about what Jake meant. He had no clue.

"Oh, come on Reece," Jake taunted him, "It's been with you for a month now."

Reece couldn't think straight. By this point, he'd been overwhelmed by feelings of anger and rage.

"Jane loved it." Jake added, giving Reece another

hint. Reece's eyes widened. The statue. Reece's fingerprints were all over it. Jake was framing him for the murder.

"You motherfucker." Reece went to make a second, hate-filled, lunge at Jake. Jake once again managed to move out of the way.

"Ah-ah-ah!" Jake said, waving the gun at Reece, "Don't worry I'll tell you all about it Reece."

Using the loaded gun in his hand, Jake pointed Reece in the direction of the sofa.

"Sit." Jake demanded. Reece, knowing he was at the disadvantage, followed Jake's instruction.

"Before I tell you how I killed Jason," Jake told him, "Let me tell you how I killed Fred and Olly."

18 FRED AND OLLY

Thursday 27th July 2017.

It was five o'clock in the afternoon. Jake had avoided taking a second drink of the whiskey, but he continued to ponder it. Jake looked down at his hands to see dry blood from punching the wall. All this rage was from Jane standing him up at the café with no warning. Jake was so full of anger and despair that he could feel it consuming him.

He decided to get himself another drink, thinking it would calm him down. He didn't want whiskey, instead, he went to the fridge and grabbed himself a beer. The more he drank, the angrier he got. After a few drinks, even though he wasn't drunk, his emotions got stronger and stronger.

By about eight o'clock, Jake's emotions were higher than ever. He snapped. Jake headed straight out, not thinking of where he would go. He went on a walk to clear his head. Whilst he was out, he stumbled upon the Fradley's arms. As he walked past, Jake saw Jane and Reece with the usual group.

'So she threw it all away just for him' Jake thought to himself, overcome with rage. Jake wanted to go in there and make Reece hurt. He struggled to stay mad at Jane. Jake stood in view for a few moments and then saw Fred and Olly in there too. A truly evil thought followed. Jake looked at the car park and saw their cars. He headed over to Olly's car and thought about what he could do. He looked around and saw that a local corner shop was open, so head headed over there for inspiration.

Jake looked through the store, trying to come up with ideas. He saw a Stanley knife for sale, which he took to the counter and purchased using cash. He'd seen about cutting brakes in action movies in the past. He just wanted to frighten Reece. To make him worry that he was going to lose someone close to him. In the same way Jake lost Jane. That'd be enough for him. Plus, hurting Fred and Olly felt right. They were the ones who caused the argument that Jake had with Jane which led to her sleeping with Reece. He blamed them just as much as the others.

Jake walked over to Olly's Mitsubishi Eclipse. He looked around and then got the flashlight on his phone so he could look for the braking system. Once he found it, he made a slight puncture hole. He saw the fluid from the brake slowly seep out of the incision he had made.

Jake took off and got away from the cars. He knew that on Thursday nights, Olly and Fred used to race down this one quiet road. Jake slowly made his way over there, knowing he had a bit of time before they would get there. He wanted to see if anything happened. He had no intentions of seriously hurting anyone. Just a minor scare.

Jake got to the road and waited for a while, hidden from sight. Eventually, he heard the sound of two loud engines. Mufflers on the exhausts. Coming in hot. The two cars raced past. A Nissan and a Mitsubishi. Fred and Olly. For the next ten minutes, the two would drive up and down the road, turning around at the round-a-bouts on either end. Jake watched as Fred's Nissan came past him, followed by Olly's Mitsubishi.

Olly wanted to get as close as he could to Fred's car. He pulled in close behind to get into Fred's slip stream, almost as if they were racing professionally. This time, he was going to overtake Fred.

Olly moved out from behind and went to brake late to get past him. Olly planted his foot onto the brake pedal, but nothing happened. He quickly removed his foot and pushed down on the pedal again, but he didn't slow down. Olly panicked for a brief moment, but that was all it took.

He ploughed into Fred's car, hitting the driver's

side head-on. Fred's car rolled and went into a frenzy, rolling three times and ending up on its roof. Olly had headbutted the steering wheel on impact, rendering him unconscious instantly. His car's momentum carried him forwards until it hit a lamp post.

Jake saw the crash from a distance and was stunned. The accident looked as if it had been ripped out of the script of an action movie. Jake never expected it to happen this way. Deep down though, beyond all the alcohol, he knew the risks he was taking. He knew what danger he was putting them in.

Jake ran straight over to Olly's car and saw he was unconscious but could hear him breathing. He then went to Fred's car, where Fred was conscious, hanging upside down. His wrist was broken from the wheel snapping away from him and his face was covered in blood.

"Jake?" Fred said, squinting through the blood dripping down into his eyes, "Is that you?"

Jake didn't say a word. He could see Fred was being held into his seat by the seat belt.

"Help me." Fred whimpered. Jake took a moment to think. His thoughts weren't clear. Alcohol and anger were clouding his judgement. Jake continued to stare at Fred.

"Jake," Fred shouted, "Fucking get me out!"

Jake continued to stare. Fred realised at that moment that Jake wasn't there to help. Fred began urgently trying to unclip his seat belt to free himself. Jake just stood and watched. Fred became more and more anxious the more he struggled to get out of the car. He just didn't have the strength.

"Look, Jake," He said, "Whatever it is, I'm sorry. But please help me."

Fred pleaded and looked into Jake's eyes. Jake reached his one hand in and put it round the back of Fred's head. Without a word, Jake slammed Fred's head against the steering wheel.

Jake heard a crack as Fred's now lifeless body remained suspended in the air, held in place by his seat belt.

Jake stood up and took a few steps back. He looked around at the scene of the accident that he had caused. Death and destruction surrounded him.

Jake looked back at Olly's car, knowing that he was still alive. Jake went up to the smashed window and could hear Olly breathing. Jake waited for a moment to see if Olly made any sort of movement. There was nothing. Jake prepared to kill Olly in a similar way to how he had killed Fred, only to stop himself. He needed someone to take the blame for Fred dying. He needed to be sure that nobody would come looking for him to put the blame on him.

Instead, Jake stepped back and looked around once more at the scene of the accident. With nobody in sight, he put his hood up and walked off down a nearby nature reserve pathway. He headed home. Along the way, Jake took off his hoodie and wiped his hands clean of any blood. He dropped the hoodie in the forest and covered it with some leaves. He knew that leaving a blood-stained hoodie in a nearby bin might raise suspicion. Obviously, he didn't want to keep it at his house, so he thought that was the best place to hide it. Once that was done, Jake continued heading home.

Jake made it home about an hour later and instantly started drinking again. He didn't get to sleep until the early hours of Friday morning. Little did he know that, by that time, Fred was already dead, and Olly had been rushed into the hospital. When Jake's emotions and alcohol mixed together, death would certainly follow.

The next morning, Jake woke up and went out on a walk. He headed past the scene where the accident occurred and could see the Police cordon still up. He looked on from a distance as the cars were being removed. Jake continued walking, stopping off at an off-licence to get some beer.

On the way back home, he headed past the scene of the accident again. This time, the road had opened back up. Jake walked over to the location where Fred's car had stopped. He looked down and noticed a small piece of debris which had been swept against the kerb to avoid any cars getting a puncture. Jake kneeled down and picked the small piece of plastic up. He looked it over and then put it into his pocket before walking away. A reminder to him of what he had done.

Jake didn't find out about Olly's death until the engagement party when Reece told him. By that point, Jake was already too far gone to even care. He was a shell of the person who he used to be.

19 JASON

Thursday 2nd November 2017

'Jane and Reece would like to announce their engagement. Party on Sunday the Fifth of November at their house. Starting at one o'clock in the afternoon and finishing at five o'clock in the evening.'

Jake looked over the post again and again. The post announcing Jane and Reece's engagement had been uploaded on Saturday. He still couldn't get over it. He drank and paced around his house thinking of what he was going to do.

Eventually, Jake decided that he was going to crash Jane and Reece's engagement party. That would be the start of his plan to hurt Reece for ruining his life and win Jane back.

He went out that afternoon to buy gifts for both Jane and Reece to 'celebrate' their engagement. He went to a small store not far from his house called 'Jennie and Morgan's.' Locally, it was known as J&M's as a homage to another famous store.

Jake browsed for a while until he saw a beautiful statue of a man and a pregnant woman.

Jake approached the counter and spoke with the cashier, whose nametag read 'Ellie.' Jake asked her if she could get the statue out of the locked glass cabinet in which it was being stored.

The cashier got the statue out for him and placed it into a box. It came to seventy pounds in total. It was expensive but worth it. This was the gift that he was planning on giving to Jane.

Jake paid in cash for the statue and left. He then decided that, instead of going straight home, he would go on a short walk. Whilst on the walk, he came across an off-licence.

Recalling Reece's alcohol issues, he knew the exact gift to buy for him. Jake went into the off-licence, which cornered two streets on a housing estate, and purchased a bottle of Whiskey.

Jake had spent a hundred pounds on the pair of them put together, which was a lot of money considering he didn't have a job and was living off the government benefits scheme. Luckily, he had money which he had been putting away for when he needed it. Although it wasn't considered an emergency, Jake decided that this was such an occasion.

Jake continued on his walk. Whilst out walking, he saw a familiar face on the other side of the road.

"Jase!" Jake shouted as he waved. Jake looked both ways to double-check that there weren't any cars coming before crossing the road. Jason paused as he waited for Jake to cross over.

"Hey mate," Jason responded, "How's it going?"

"As well as it can." Jake replied. Jason's facial expression changed in an instant.

"I take it that you saw the announcement then from Reece and Jane." Jason said back to Jake.

"I did," Jake nodded.

"How're you holding up?" Jason replied which a sympathetic look on his face, "Can't be easy."

Jake shook his head, "It's been tough mate, I'm not going to lie."

Jason saw the expression of sadness on Jake's face. He looked down and checked his watch, then looked back up at Jake.

"I've got an hour of spare time now mate," Jason said, putting his arm on Jake's shoulder, "Do you fancy getting a drink?"

"Yeah," Jake said, "Can do mate."

They didn't head to the Fradley's arms. Instead, they headed to another local bar which was closer to where they were at the time. The two went in, got their drinks, and sat down at a table.

They had some general conversation for a while and caught up with each other. Eventually, they moved on to talk about how Jake felt about the whole situation with Jane and Reece.

His feelings could have been summarised in one

word – shit – but Jake dragged it out for a while instead. Jake drank his fair share of alcohol in that hour. By the time the hour had passed, Jake was drunk. Not because he was a lightweight but because of how quickly he had drank them.

"Jake," Jason said, checking his watch, "I think it's time we leave."

Jake swayed at the table for a moment, "But why?"

"You're pissed mate," Jason replied chuckling, "Come on, I'll walk you home."

Jake grabbed his wallet, phone and keys off the table and the two of them headed for the door. Jake swayed a bit, but Jason was there to support him. Jason slowly walked him out of the pub and then asked Jake for his postcode. Jason put the postcode into the maps software he had on his phone and then slowly directed Jake back to his house.

Once the pair got back to Jake's, Jason guided him to the kitchen and got him a glass of water. Jake put the statue and the bottle of whiskey on the table.

"Am I going to be okay to leave you?" Jason asked Jake, putting the glass onto the table.

"Go ahead," Jake replied, "Everyone else already has."

Jason needed to leave, otherwise, he would have offered to stay. Sheepishly, he put his head down and headed towards the kitchen door which led out into the hallway. Jake saw Jason leaving and his mind just switched.

"I thought we were friends." Jake said, standing

up. The anger was clearly visible to Jason on his face.

"We are Jake," Jason replied, "I've got to go though mate. I've got things that need doing."

"So why offer to stay?" Jake asked, feeling a mix of both rejection and anger which wasn't helped by the amount of alcohol flowing through his system.

"I didn't Jake," Jason replied, "I asked if I was going to be okay to leave you and you said go ahead."

Jake clenched his fist.

"Chill out man," Jason told Jake, putting both hands out and signalling a calm-down gesture with them. He was starting to get concerned about Jake's change in personality.

"I'm calm," Jake replied, "I'm calm."

The two had a stare-off for a moment, and then Jason headed for the front door. As he turned around, Jake picked the statue up by the pregnant lady and rushed towards Jason.

Before Jason even had a chance to react to the sound of Jake's frantic footsteps, he felt a sharp pain across the back of his head. It sent him that dizzy that he dropped straight to the floor, banging his head off a nearby table in the process.

Jake was rageful. Rageful but frozen at the same time. He waited for Jason to get up. He never did. Blood seeped out of the two open wounds on Jason's head. One from the back of his head. One from the side of his head near his left eye. Jake slowly realised the gravity of his actions. Jake looked down at the statue and saw it was covered in blood. Jake knelt down and put his finger to Jason's neck, checking his pulse. Nothing.

Jake stood back up and looked down at Jason. He could help Jason but that would lead to the truth coming out about what had just happened. Instead, Jake headed straight to the sink and started to clean the statue.

As he was cleaning it under the tap, a piece chipped away from the corner. He looked at the chip for a moment in disappointment. Then, he cleaned away the tiny splatters and grains of blood and wrapped it up in a towel to dry it. Jake then headed to the cupboard and got some latex gloves out.

Jake doubled-gloved his hands, layering one on top of the other. He slowly moved over to Jason's lifeless corpse and checked again for a pulse. He waited for two minutes. Nothing. Jason was truly dead.

Jake, surprisingly, wasn't panicked by any of this though. Instead of stressing about what to do, he took deep breaths and calmed himself down, regaining some sobriety. Not much of it though.

Jake wrapped up Jason's body in bin bags and used cello tape to seal the bags together. He wrapped the bags in multiple layers and even hummed a little tune as he did it. Jake felt no regret. Although, he was justifying it to himself over and over again in his head.

He moved the body to the back porch of the house and then stepped out into the garden. He walked around in his garden for a bit and looked for anywhere which he could put Jason's body temporarily without arousing much suspicion from his neighbours. He looked about for a while and then thought up an idea which was psychotically genius.

Jake headed to his shed and emptied it out. Lawnmower. Rake. Spades. Power tools. Anything that was in there, he took into the house. Jake then put the body by the back door in a space which none of his neighbours could see from their rear windows. Jake took his gloves off and went upstairs. He had a warm shower and headed for bed. Jake set an alarm for two o'clock in the morning. He put his head on the pillow and closed his eyes.

Jake was soon awoken by his alarm going off. He reached over to his bedside table and checked his phone. Two o'clock in the morning. Jake got up and got into a dark-coloured tracksuit. He headed downstairs, taking a bin bag filled with his clothes which he had worn when he killed Jason. Jake put some latex gloves on and headed out to the garden. Jason was still there. Not that he would have been able to go far anyway.

Jake lifted Jason's deadweight, lifeless corpse off the ground and walked towards the shed, which he had purposely left open to save time and to avoid making any sound which would alert his neighbours.

Jake put Jason's body in the shed and shut the door, securing it with a padlock. He took the key out and kept it with him. He headed back into the house and put the key on the side in the kitchen. Whilst in there, he took his gloves off and got changed again.

He had another shower and then poured himself a drink.

Now all that was left was to dispose of Jason. He already knew what he was going to do with the murder weapon. Jake covered his tracks well. Years of watching crime documentaries was helping him.

Saturday 4th November 2017

Jake waited a few days and then started to dismantle the shed, putting pieces into black bin bags which he then stacked on top of Jason's body. He reversed the car up to the gate, laid some tarpaulin in his boot, and then propped the gate open with a brick. Jake put the bags of wood and Jason's corpse into a wheelbarrow, which he then took down towards his car and moved each item, and Jason's body, one by one. The last item he put in there was a shovel.

As Jake finished loading the car, one of his neighbours came out of the house. Jake shut the boot to avoid any suspicion.

"Hi Jake," His neighbour said, "Haven't seen you in a while. How've you been?"

"Hi mate," Jake responded, "It's not been great. I don't know whether you know but me and Jane have split up."

"Oh, that's terrible news," The neighbour replied, "How are you coping?"

"I'm taking each day as it comes," Jake told his neighbour, "Anyways, I'm just in the middle of packing a few things up. Sorry to dash off."

"No worries," The neighbour said, smiling at Jake, "In the meantime if you need anything, you know where we are."

Jake nodded and smiled at his friendly neighbour before turning around and heading back into the house, making sure to lock his car.

Once everything was in place, Jake waited until the nighttime and then left the house when it was dark. He headed to the local forestry where he parked up in a layby which wasn't far from where he wanted to go.

Jake got out of the car and checked to see if anyone was around. Empty. Jake headed to the boot and opened it up. He picked up the shovel and lay it on top of Jason's body. Jake then picked Jason up and started carrying him into the forest. He could feel the cold coming off Jason's body through his gloves.

He lay Jason down and started to dig, his torch being held in his mouth. Jake dug and dug for hours. It was still dark by the time that he had finished digging the shallow grave.

He rolled Jason's body in and lay some of the wood on top of it. He'd cleaned it all down and worn gloves when dismantling the shed to avoid getting his fingerprints on it.

Jake piled the soil back on top and then patted it down to try to make it look a bit more natural. It was clear that the ground had been disturbed but it was the best he could manage.

Jake then put the shovel and the remaining bags

back inro his boot and drove home. The next day, he dropped the bags, shovel, and clothes off at the local landfill waste site. Then that was it. Just like that, any trace of Jason vanished.

20 REECE

Reece was frozen to the spot. He couldn't believe what he had heard. Jake had killed Jason, Fred, and Jane. Not to mention that he was somewhat responsible for Olly's death too. Jake had gone crazy. Insane.

"You fucking bastard!" Reece yelled as he went to lunge at Jake again. Jake didn't say a word. He pointed the gun at Reece once more and aimed it at his head.

"Back up Reece," Jake said firmly, "You're not going to be able to get any revenge if you're dead."

"I'll take you with me asshole," Reece grunted back. He launched himself at Jake in a blind fit of rage. Reece launched for Jake's waist, hoping to tackle him into the wall. Jake calmly stepped aside, which caused Reece to bundle into the wall, banging his head and shoulder before dropping to the floor. He was in pain. Both physically and mentally. That wouldn't stop him though. Reece wasn't ready to give up.

He got himself back to his feet and turned around to face Jake. Without saying a word, Reece charged like a bull. He lifted his right hand into the air, fist clenched, and struck towards Jake. Jake ducked under the punch and hit Reece in the stomach with the handle of the gun. Reece was winded and stumbled to the floor.

"Don't get up Reece," Jake replied, cocking the gun, "It's not going to end well for you."

Reece got straight to his feet, "You wouldn't do it, I can tell."

"What makes you think that?" Jake replied, shaking the gun slightly to show he was pointing it at Reece's head.

"Because you'd have done it by now," Reece told Jake, "You're used to it anyway. You're used to killing."

Jake's head dipped slightly. He was clearly ashamed. Reece spotted an opportunity.

"Yeah, you're nothing but a killer," Reece said, seeing Jake's expression start to change, "A killer who killed the love of his life."

Reece noticed Jake mood changing. This wasn't just a physical fight but a mental one too.

"You couldn't have loved her. What kind of person murders the woman he loves?" Reece continued to talk at Jake, starting to edge closer. "I'll tell you who does that."

Jake froze for a second. Reece edged closer. Then, he spotted his chance.

"A coward," He told Jake. Intent on seizing the opportunity, Reece hurled forwards, reaching for the gun. Jake snapped back into focus and moved out of the way, hitting Reece in the back with the gun. Reece let out a yelp in pain and stumbled to the floor once more.

"Why are you doing this?" Reece shouted in agony, rolling over to face Jake.

"Because of you," Jake snapped back, "You ruined my life!"

"Oh, grow up Jake," Reece shouted, "How did I do that?"

"You know full well," Jake replied, calming his voice, "You took Jane from me. The only thing. The only person I cared about in the world."

"Says the one who killed her," Reece replied, "If you hadn't have had your outburst then none of this would have happened."

"Don't you blame this on me," Jake shouted as he gritted his teeth together in anger, "This was your fault."

"Yeah okay," Reece responded, "Blame someone else. This little outburst will be over soon, and you'll realise what you've done."

Reece targeted Jake's ego. Their time apart meant that Reece was easily able to spot the shift in Jake's confidence. He could see by the way Jake held himself. The confidence he had in admitting he had killed Jane, Jason and the others, Jake was proud of what he had done. Which told Reece that Jake's ego was just getting bigger and bigger.

"You think this is an outburst?" Jake asked.

"Exactly that," Reece told him, "It didn't sound like you actually wanted or meant to kill any of them. You lost control."

"Bullshit." Jake snapped.

"I'm on the mark though, aren't I?" Reece replied, slowly getting back up to his feet, "All of this was one accident, one convenience, after the other."

Jake went to shout back but held his tongue before he did. He smirked.

"I know what you're doing," Jake replied, "But let me correct you. This was all planned. I wanted to put you in the worst pain possible. Then, I planned on seeing you be faced with a dilemma and a losing situation."

Reece looked at Jake confused.

"See, I know you all too well Reece," Jake said, "And now I'm going to face you with two options."

Jake walked over to him and outstretched his hand which he held the gun in. Reece snatched it away and pointed it at Jake. Jake remained calm. In control.

"Option one is that you turn me in. You tell the police when they arrive what I did, and I go to prison. As soon as I get to prison, I'll be dead in a week. I won't get any punishment because I've wanted to die for months now. I'll get rewarded instead." Jake told

Reece. Reece's facial expression turned to anger which grew deeper inside him knowing that Jake was right. Knowing that justice wouldn't be served. Reece wanted Jake to pay for what he had done.

"But you came here for revenge. So let me tell you about option two. You kill me today and you follow in my footsteps. You become a killer. You get justice but serve a life sentence in prison for my murder and Jason's murder. After all, you've had the murder weapon this entire time." Jake replied. There was no way Reece could go down for Jason's murder. The body hadn't even been found. Reece never thought about that though. His judgement was clouded by anger and rage which he focused on Jake.

"You'll spend the rest of your days in prison. Either way, I win. Your life is finished right here and now," Jake told Reece, "You won't come back from this."

Reece stood there for a moment. He looked down at the gun and back up at Jake, pondering his next move.

"So, what's it gonna be Reece?" Jake asked.

Reece put the gun to Jake's head and held it there for a few seconds. His finger itched to pull the trigger. His head was telling him to do it, but his heart was saying otherwise.

"There it is." Jake replied, closing his eyes, and waiting for the shot that would finally set him free. Reece held the gun to Jake's head for a few seconds but didn't fire. Jake opened his eyes.

"What're you waiting for?" Jake shouted, desperate to push Reece over the edge, "DO IT!"

"No," Reece replied, lowering the gun, "You're already dead inside anyway, you don't get off this easy."

Jake saw the faint glisten of blue lights getting brighter and brighter. Reece didn't know that, when Jake went to the toilet earlier, he made a well-timed call to the Police.

Jake looked Reece dead in the eyes. A cold look that sent a shiver straight down Reece's spine.

"You're done." He said to Reece, completely void of emotion.

Jake made a sudden movement to his waistband behind his back, as if he was grabbing something. Reece, expecting that Jake was about to kill him, quickly raised the gun back to Jake's head and pulled the trigger. The loud bang of the gunshot echoed throughout the house.

Time stopped still for Reece as he watched Jake's body dropped to the floor. Reece looked on in horror as Jake's corpse lay there staring back at him. It was only then that Reece noticed the flashing blue lights illuminating the room. Police.

Reece panicked and dropped the gun as the officers smashed down the front door. Not knowing what to do, he ran straight for the back of the house. It was fight or flight and Reece knew he wouldn't win this fight. So, he had to run.

"Police!" An officer shouted as he spotted Reece

running, "Stop right there!"

He opened the back door which led out into the garden and started jumping fences. Reece wasn't planning on going down for murder. He went to jump the last fence to see officers waiting on the other side. Reece dropped back down and broke through the other fence at the end of the garden. He started running down the back of the houses towards a nearby nature reserve. Reece carried on running, losing his breath but not his will to carry on with life.

He ran down the path, glancing behind and seeing a herd of police officers chasing after him. Reece took a left turn and ran into the forest. Officers continued chasing behind. They weren't close enough yet to deploy a taser onto him.

Reece carried on sprinting through the small forest and ran into a nearby alleyway where he hid in the trees and bushes. He could hear the pounding footsteps of officers running past as he remained hidden, much like Jake did as a child when he hid from Reece.

He waited until he was seemingly out of sight, then stepped out. He carried on through the forest, eventually emerging onto a pathway on the other side. Reece continued down the path. Thinking he had lost the officers, he unzipped his hoodie and threw it into a nearby bush before heading out onto the main road. He crossed straight over and continued to walk.

He walked for about twenty seconds. Then, he heard the sound of the Police helicopter above him.

FOLLOW IN MY FOOTSTEPS

Knowing they could see him, Reece carried on sprinting. He ran down a road onto a nearby business park, still being followed by the Police helicopter. Suddenly, two unmarked Police cars flew around the corner and stopped directly ahead of Reece. Another two unmarked cars blocked the road behind him. The firearms officers got out and pointed their guns at Reece.

"On your stomach, now!" The officers demanded. Conceding defeat, Reece lay down and put his hands out to the side. He felt the officers grab his arms and force them into handcuffs.

"You are under arrest for murder. You do not have to say anything, but it may harm your defence if you do not mention, when questioned, something which you may later rely on in court. Anything you do say may be given in evidence." The officer told Reece, who was completely silent.

Reece was searched and then escorted to the Police car, where he sat in the back and the officers started driving to the nearby custody suite. Reece looked at the sat nav on the officer's phone. Ten minutes until arrival.

21 THAT'S HOW IT HAPPENED

Officers remained at the scene of the shooting. Flash after flash from the cameras of the forensic officers helped them to capture the scene. Jake's body was photographed, his clothes were seized, and then he was placed into a bag and zipped up.

The case sat with one of the more experienced detectives on the team. He looked over the pictures of the blood-stained walls and the body of Jake Lawson. He reviewed statements and the evidence he had. Then, he and his partner headed to custody to get ready to interview their prime suspect. Reece Stephenson.

Reece

Reece lay in the cell facing the ceiling. The cold, plain walls made him feel even lonelier. The only time he was taken out of his cell was to have his photograph and fingerprints taken.

Eventually, his cell door was opened, and two detectives came into view. Reece sat up.

"Solicitor's here," The detective told Reece, nodding his head in the direction he intended on taking Reece.

Reece walked out of his cell, putting on his pumps, and followed them to a room where he went into consultation with his solicitor. The fact that he had run from the police hadn't really helped his cause. He was advised to go "no comment" and was then taken to an interview room.

The recording started. Reece could feel the drops of sweat pouring down his forehead. He initially answered their questions with the words "no comment."

Reece felt like this was a nightmare that he couldn't wake up from. Guilt and despair filled his thoughts as he started to come to terms with what had happened. Then, a question hit him which changed his answers completely.

"Did you kill Jake Lawson?" The detective asked.

"No comment." Reece replied, looking down at the table and letting out a huff of disappointment and disbelief.

The room fell silent for a second. A second which, to Reece, felt like an eternity. Then, Reece spoke again.

"I shot him." Reece told the two detectives sat

opposite him. His solicitor nudged him to remind him to say "no comment."

"Why did you shoot him, Reece?" The detective replied.

"He reached for something, I thought he was going to kill me." Reece answered.

"The gun was yours though, wasn't it?" The detective asked.

"Yes," Reece replied, "But Jake had it pointed to my head."

"Your prints were the only ones lifted off the gun," The detective replied, "And Jake didn't have anything behind his back when his body was searched. How do you account for that?"

"I," Reece stuttered. He wanted to give an answer, but he couldn't think of anything which they would believe. In Reece's eyes, they made their minds up before they came into the interview.

"No comment." Reece said as he slumped back down in his seat.

The detectives got up and left the room after finishing the rest of their questions, to which Reece answered with "no comment." He wanted to tell them the truth, but it was clear to him that they wouldn't believe him. He'd have to save it for court.

That's what he did. The court day rolled around, and Reece was given his opportunity to defend himself. He explained his side of the story, telling them that Jake killed Jane, Fred, and Jason. This sparked a new line of enquiry for officers as Jason's body had not yet been recovered. Jason's body, in fact, wouldn't be found for another five years, when a man doing some metal detecting would pick up on a screw and stumble upon the remains whilst digging for treasure.

Reece was being further investigated for the deaths of Fred and Jane, as he was able to provide details which had not yet been made public. He wasn't charged with them in the end due to evidential difficulties. They looked into the fact that Jake could have killed him but there wasn't enough evidence to say that he had. Not that it would matter. Jake was dead and buried.

After days of court trials and hearings, Reece was found guilty of the murder of Jake Lawson. The sentencing day came around and Reece was sentenced to thirty years. Reece was escorted through the prison and to his new home. He was put into a cold, poorly lit room. One bed where he put his belongings which he was allowed. The prison officer slammed the door behind him, sending a chill down his spine caused by the noise and the breeze off the door.

Reece's life was now officially over. He was deemed a murderer. He had well and truly, followed in Jake's footsteps.

22 EPILOGUE

Jane woke up in the morning to her alarm. She cleaned her teeth and got her two children ready for school. The three of them all sat together in the brightly-coloured kitchen. They all laughed and joked for about ten minutes until her husband, Alex, came down the stairs. He had been out late drinking the night before.

Alex entered the room wearing his dressing gown and slippers, with the smell of booze following behind.

"Morning," Jane said, standing up to get him a drink, "Nice of you to join us for once."

He rolled his eyes, "Don't start."

"Are you going to work today or are you 'off sick'

again?" Jane asked rhetorically. She already knew what the answer was going to be.

Alex grabbed some milk out of the fridge, poured it into a glass and headed back up to bed. Jane didn't stay in the house much longer after that. She finished the school run and went straight to work. She had a busy day ahead of her.

Just before her lunch, Jane was arguing with Alex on the phone. That morning was the final straw in their collapsing marriage. She had tried to save it, but Alex's alcoholic traits had broken it. She had tried and tried but she couldn't manage it any longer.

She sat in the break room on her lunch, receiving text after text from Alex apologising. She replied to some but not all. Just then, a colleague came in.

"You look like shit," The colleague said, "Problems with Alex again?"

"I've just had enough with him now," Jane replied, "I've tried to fix things, but I can't deal with it anymore."

"Why don't you go home?" Her colleague replied, pouring some hot water from the kettle into her mug, "I'm sure work will understand."

"I might do," Jane replied, agreeing with her colleague, "I'll just get this next appointment out of the way. He's been dying to see someone all week, but no one would see him apparently."

"What's his name?" Her colleague replied.

"Some guy name Reece Stephenson," Jane answered.

She finished off her drink and headed into her office and awaited her next appointment.

Reece

Reece had a really tough time in prison. He spent his days desperately trying to convince everyone he spoke to that it was self-defence. The more he told people, the more he felt ignored and rejected. Nobody listened to him. Nobody believed him. The rejection slowly started impacting on his mental health. He could feel himself drifting away, becoming a shell of the man he once was. He made various applications to see a therapist, eventually managing to get an appointment.

Reece was getting more and more irritated. He wanted to lash out but was fearful that he would just end up the same as Jake. He couldn't make any friends in the prison, and he never got any contact from the outside world. All his friends were dead. His only reason to keep going was that, if he killed himself, Jake would have really won. The longer he stayed alive though, the more he suffered.

Reece got attacked a lot in the prison as well. As he wasn't the popular one anymore. He had nobody to stick up for him. His experience of prison had started to give him a true insight into how Jake must have felt. He couldn't justify Jake's actions, but the more Reece adjusted to his new life, the more he understood Jake.

He sat there one day with a razor, a toothbrush,

and some tape. He'd accumulated these quietly whilst in prison. He snapped the end of the toothbrush and made a makeshift weapon. A shiv. That way, the next time someone attacked him, he could defend himself.

He kept the shiv in his underwear. In a place which would make it difficult to be found if he were to be searched. Having the shiv with him made him feel a bit safer knowing that he could defend himself if needed. It gave him a form of mental comfort.

Reece was resting on his bed when the cell door opened. It was his turn to see the therapist. He was searched and escorted to the room where he would be able to sit down and speak with the therapist. A nice, polite young lady with a ponytail. Coincidentally, her name was Jane.

He sat down in the chair opposite her and the two got to talking. Reece started explaining his version of events and then went on to say how he was feeling depressed. The therapist sat writing on bits of paper and occasionally checked her phone whenever it pinged. Every time she did, Reece paused. The more he continued to pause, the more irritated he got.

Eventually, Reece snapped. Jane's phone pinged again. She picked it up to check it, rolling her eyes at the sight of yet another text from Alex. That was the last straw for Reece though.

"Are you gonna fucking listen to me or keep playing with your phone?" Reece shouted, demanding an answer.

"I'm sorry Reece," She replied, putting her phone

down and trying to remain as polite as possible, "Please, do carry on."

"Nobody listens to me in this place," He shouted, "Not one person. I'm sick of it. All I want is for someone to hear me."

"Well take a deep breath and tell me," She responded, "I'm listening."

"No, you're not," He answered, "You're too busy playing on your phone. It's your job to listen."

"I just had to check it," She told him, trying to calm him down, "I'm sorry."

"No, you just have to do your job," Reece stood up, "What do I have to do to get someone to listen?"

"Reece, please sit down," The therapist said in a calm voice, despite the rising tensions, "I'll listen if you sit down."

"I know," Reece said, pulling the shiv out of his underwear, "I'll make people listen."

Reece lunged towards the therapist who screamed out for the guards. The guards launched into the room and instantly took hold of Reece. It was too late.

The shiv was hanging out of the therapist's neck, severing an artery, and causing blood to spurt out which painted the room red. She put her hand to her neck as she slowly dropped to the floor. Guards rushed in to support Jane, but it was too late. She lost too much blood in such a short space of time. Within minutes, she was dead.

Reece was dragged down to segregation. He just

laughed on the way down.

"Maybe now you'll all fucking listen," Reece shouted as he laughed.

Reece was thrown into the cell and strip-searched. The door was shut behind him. He was even more isolated now than ever. He was isolated for months, receiving mental health assessments through a hatch. He couldn't be trusted to be around other prisoners at the time.

About two years passed until Reece was deemed fit to return to the normal cell block. When he was returned, he was convicted for Jane's murder. He never realized her name until the trial, which made it all the worse for him.

Reece spent another few years in prison. Not speaking to anyone from the outside world or seeing anyone. That was until one day. Reece was told he had a visitor. He was confused. Nobody had visited him the whole time he was in the prison. Not a soul. So why now?

He sat at the table opposite the unfamiliar face. A big-built gentleman, who was wearing a tee shirt and some jeans.

"Hello Reece," The male said, "Can I have a moment of your time?"

And so, Reece sat down. Eager to hear what this mystery man had to say.

ABOUT THE AUTHOR

D.J. WADDISON is a new, young, author from Staffordshire, England. Whilst only having released his first book (Follow in my Footsteps) in 2023 at just twenty-three years old, DJ loves to write fictional stories covering a blend of genres in his spare time. These typically include; mystery, crime, and thriller. He also enjoys sneaking in bits of comic relief into his stories where he can as well as making references to family and friends.

Facebook @d.j.waddison
Instagram @d.j.waddison
Twitter @dj_waddison
Website – https://waddisondj.wixsite.com/official

FOLLOW IN MY FOOTSTEPS

D.J. WADDISON

DON'T FOLLOW IN MY FOOTSTEPS THE PREQUEL TO FOLLOW IN MY FOOTSTEPS.

COMING 2024.

Printed in Great Britain
by Amazon